Lady IN Lace

L.H. WILLIAMS

About the Authors

Dear Reader,

If you've read our first two books, *Saving Dee* and *The Penny Scam*, you know that we coauthor *The Dee Chronicles*. We are a young-at-heart married couple who found each other again after many years apart. We discovered that we shared a shared love of writing that began more than fifty years ago when we studied with our much-loved English teacher, Doris Pock.

Over the years Heyward and I have been avid readers. I love Regency romance, and he usually reaches for adventure books. When we began to write, we thought we should have some fun with it. So, if you find our characters and plots to be somewhat "over the top," you're right. Our heroine is beautiful, our hero is rich and handsome, and our crooks and bad guys are downright dirty dogs who always manage to screw up! That's the way we like it.

We have fun writing, and we hope you enjoy reading *Lady in Lace,* the third book of *The Dee Chronicles*. While it continues the story of Dee and Jared, it adds some new characters, including Mary Rose Benefacio, whose hatred of Dee fuels a crazed plot to bring her down.

We'd especially like to thank two friends who are our *beta readers*, Barb Piccirillo and Linda Logan Bird, for their willingness to read and critique our early draft manuscripts. Special thanks to our developmental editor, Nikki Busch, not only for her editing talent, but also for her continued support, advice, and friendship.

Meanwhile, we are hard at work on our fourth book, entitled *Forever Yours, My Darling.*

All the best,
Louise and Heyward Williams

Email: thedeechronicles@gmail.com

Book 1 – Saving Dee

Dee Milan knows she's been unlucky in love, having traded in her dreams for the glitz and glamor of marrying a wealthy man. But what she doesn't know is that she'll be even unluckier if her scheming husband Steve—a powerful, ruthless brute—gets away with his latest plan for her.

When a mysterious, handsome stranger with brains and a hard body shows up on the sailboat docked next to her yacht, Dee discovers her luck just might change.

Jared Herreshoff is brilliant at uncovering fraud, making international deals, and investigating people of interest. He's a master at navigating complex problems and navigating his beloved sailboat *Chauffeuse*. Although he couldn't save his first love, he's faced with a second chance when he's asked to protect Dee.

Can Jared save Dee from a life of bad decisions, deception, and danger?

With high-spirited adventure that goes from Miami Beach to the Bahamas and then to Las Vegas, *Saving Dee* is a wild ride of romance, humor, and excitement.

Book 2 – The Penny Scam

With her thug of an ex-husband out of the picture, Dee Milan thinks she's finally safe in the arms of her new love and protector, Jared Herreshoff. They're ready to move on, but are her ex-husband's "business associates"?

While Jared and his security company, Protek, are busy keeping Dee safe, a new assignment has Protek's sleuths stumped, and the only one who can help them solve it is an unlikely ally— young David Jesse Owen, aka DJ—a wily, eccentric computer hacker who steals pennies from the rich and gives to the poor while using junk food to fuel his operation.

Dee, Jared, and the Protek gang have big ambitions in the romance and career departments. But they'll have to dodge a few bullets (or worse), don a few more costumes, and travel to New York, Boston, Newark, and even Saskatchewan, if they want to hit their goals. Can love survive another attack?

Book 3 – Lady in Lace

Dee and Jared think they have it all, including her successful art gallery, his security firm, and their house in the country. But old hatreds die hard, and one member of their old rival's family has it in for Dee – Joseph's daughter. Mary Rose is jealous of Dee and concocts a scheme she thinks will bring her down "in a blaze of glory."

While she fumes and plots, Jared's team defies the odds to bring home a kidnapped teen who is headed for child slavery unless they can save her in time.

And, when Jared decides to take his beloved Chauffeuse on a boat race to Bermuda, he encounters a tough situation that puts his crew in danger.

Jared and Dee can't be everywhere at once and resolve everything alone, so they enlist the help of their Protek team to solve the complex problems that threaten their happiness. And, as luck will have it, sometimes when you aren't even looking, romance and other good things happen along the way.

Prologue

MARY ROSE WOKE UP GROGGILY and rubbed her eyes. Her head ached and at first she couldn't remember where she was. Then she realized she was in her own bed in her own apartment.

But she wasn't alone.

She rolled over and looked at the swarthy man lying beside her. She didn't even remember his name—if she had ever known it.

She was disgusted with herself and everything she had become since Jonathan's death, as she now thought of what happened that fateful day.

She reached for her cell phone and dialed a number. It was answered immediately. "Yes?"

"Come here and remove this person from my apartment. Convince him he was never here and didn't spend the night. Make him believe it would be better if he forgot all about me. Make sure he understands completely."

"Yes, Miss Benefacio." And the line went dead.

She plodded into the bathroom and turned on the shower. Afterwards, she felt a little cleaner but the memories of what she had been doing the past few months left a stench in her mind. She was in the kitchen making coffee when she heard a commotion in the bedroom. There was a surprised "Who the hell are you?" followed by the sound of blows and cries of pain— and then the front door slammed shut.

I have to stop this, she thought to herself.

It was an epiphany to her although she didn't even know what that word meant.

I need to see my priest.

She dressed quickly, went to church and slipped into the confessional, where she was welcomed with open arms.

"Come, my child, God's forgiveness awaits."

She sat quietly for a few moments while the priest waited patiently.

Finally, she said, "I have sinned, Father, and there is no way I can stop myself. I know who and what I am. There is no forgiveness for me. This is my last confession."

Then she stood up and left the booth.

Chapter 1

The Benefactor

THE SHEER MENTION OF "YOUNG Italian woman" brings to mind images of olive skin, lustrous dark hair, sultry eyes, and a buxom figure. Unfortunately, this was not the case with Mary Rose Benefacio. Although she was slim, none of the other adjectives applied to her. Her chest was unimpressive, her lips thin and tight set, and her color ran to sallow, not olive. Her hair lacked the dark, bouncy curls, so she kept it cut short, like a cap around her plain face. Expensive clothes and well-applied makeup made some inroads, but they would never be enough to give Mary Rose the look she so desired.

On this first warm evening in May of 2010, Mary Rose sat on the broad, open terrace of her brand-new apartment in Boston's West End and lit a cigarette—which she abruptly put out. She knew she shouldn't smoke, but it was a hard habit to break. She poured a whiskey and soda from her well-stocked bar and tried to convince herself to make dinner. With her feet up on the cushioned footstool of the patio set, she leaned back to admire the river view. She hadn't had this apartment for long, so it was still sparsely furnished inside, but given that it was almost summer, she began with the costly wrought-iron furniture. She knew she couldn't move too far away from her father, but she had known instinctively she could no longer cohabitate with him in the dark brownstone that had been the family home for almost fifty years.

She had been witness to her father's downhill slide ever since her brother Jonathan's death a year and a half before. Yes, Joseph was in his late seventies, she thought, but men that age often had many good years ahead of them. Her father, unfortunately, was not one of them. Although there was nothing physically wrong with him—that is, no specific illness—he was dying of a broken heart. Joseph seemed to have lost interest in life and wanted nothing more to do with his business.

Mary Rose and her father had settled into a comfortable routine. Every weekday morning at ten, she would arrive at the brownstone to have breakfast with him. She would coax him into eating his one piece of toast with a soft-boiled egg and chat with him as he downed two cups of strong coffee. In her softest manner, she would fill him in on the details of their various businesses and wait quietly, as he pondered those details before he walked her through the next steps she was to take.

Since she was a fast learner, this had become somewhat of a formality as the weeks turned into months. But Joseph was her touchstone, and without him, she had little motivation to continue the business. But, of course, she had no choice. They were family—and family was involved in the business until there was no one left to run it. So, like it or not, she knew that all of this was now on her shoulders. After breakfast, she would consult with the housekeeper about his dinner and then take leave of her father to conduct her business throughout the city and beyond.

She liked to travel and found more and more reasons to fly to New York. While she was away, she could count on the housekeeper to fill in for her, but she was careful never to be away for more than a day or two.

And even though her life was sometimes lonely as hell, Mary Rose was not one to wallow in her sorrow. Like her nemesis, Dee, she had a business plan. Maybe it wasn't housed in a pink laptop, written in a cloth-covered designer notebook, or organized in a spreadsheet—but she knew what she had to do. Businesses that didn't produce enough revenue were cut, or cut loose, leaving them to be run by people who used to work for her father. These people now ran their own operations, and some of them couldn't believe their good fortunes. Others ran theirs into the ground, but Mary Rose didn't take them back. She was down to a few core businesses that were producing money, and down to a few trusted minions who didn't care if the reins of power had switched from Joseph to Mary, but they respected her for her business sense and her ruthlessness. They knew she was a force to be reckoned with and took care to make money for her—and for themselves.

Of course, the death of Dee's ex-husband, Steve Milan, had meant the end of the computer parts and information import-export business. He had run the business alone, and his few assistants, being judged useless, had been dropped from the payroll without a backward glance. Cut your losses, she'd thought. The security and bodyguard business was going strong, as was their interest in food transport and distribution. But she was, in a word, antsy, and thought more and more about starting something new. But what?

Alone in her new apartment—and alone with her thoughts—she would daydream about what she would do if the sky really was the limit, and she could do whatever she wanted, what she loved, and it would make her richer than God. But she kept drawing blanks. And then she'd get busy again and put her dreams on hold as she dealt with the day-to-day of her petty crooks, badasses, street thugs, and hustlers.

One morning, after breakfast with Joseph, Mary Rose simply called a cab and asked the driver to take her to the airport. She had only her handbag with her and no meeting to attend. Two hours later, she found herself standing across the street from Galleria D looking into the bright and shiny windows of another world. There was Dee, as gorgeous and as blonde as ever.

And something snapped in Mary Rose.

Chapter 2

Lucia Castorini

L UCY, WHOSE REAL NAME WAS Lucia Castorini, was just getting out of class at the North Boston High School for the Gifted. Barely five feet tall, she was slim, leggy, and pretty. It was unusual for an Italian girl to be blonde and blue eyed, so her father had kidded her, telling her that a Viking had his way with her great-great-great grandmother on one of his voyages of plunder and conquest in the Mediterranean. She giggled at the thought. Did her great-great-great grandmother fight back tooth and nail? Lucy loved to imagine what *she* would have done so long ago.

She chatted with her friends in front of the old brick school, hugged her books to her chest, and headed down the street toward home. She knew she would make the varsity cheerleading team next year, and so did most of the boys in her class. She also knew she could have her pick of them.

It was a beautiful day, she thought; the sky was blue, it wasn't too hot out, and the birds were singing. She smiled at the trees around her. She was happy with her boyfriend Daniel and believed he truly loved her. Of course, he was starting to get frisky and she'd have to rein him in, especially since she'd already let him feel her 'titties.' She giggled when she thought about the first time he called them that. Well, they were large and pointy, and she'd watched lots of boys look down at her chest with interest.

But Daniel was special. He could look into her eyes, reach

around behind her back and unsnap her bra with one hand, which totally amazed her. She giggled again and hugged her books closer to her chest. What a wonderful day! She remembered that last Saturday she had almost lost her virginity in the back seat of his father's BMW. It was a close call; she had stopped him just in time. Should she let him do it? Did she want to be a virgin all her life? She was fourteen, almost fifteen. Half of her friends weren't virgins anymore and only one of them had gotten preggy. Maybe next weekend? She'd have to think about it.

From the inside of a nondescript black SUV, two men watched as the high school girls emerged from the building. "Там, это один" said one to the other. "Da," came the response. They followed her down the street, looked for a good place to stop, and found it at the corner of the park. What they didn't notice— or perhaps even care about—was the homeless man propped up against a tree, in plain sight.

Lucy walked along as if in a trance, still deep in thought over her boyfriend. Of course, her parents didn't like him because he wasn't Italian or even Catholic, but his father was a politician and a sharp businessman, so that might make it all right.

Suddenly, Lucy was grabbed from behind. She dropped her books and tried to scream, but there was a funny-smelling cloth pressed against her face... and then her world went black.

Chapter 3

Weekend in the Country

ALL DEE HAD EVER WANTED was a job in the New York City art world and a loving husband. In fact, after years of seeming to get further and further away from those goals, she was now happier than she could ever have imagined. She and Jared were so much in love that everyone who saw them together commented on it. And they were true soul mates, partners, lovers, friends, and, yes, adventurers. When they could get away from business, they would sail, hike, work out, or swim. It didn't matter what they did, as long as they were together.

It had been a busy week in New York City for Dee at Galleria D. Jared had been in New York and then gone to Boston. He had kept up by phone with Melanie, who ran Protek, the security company in which he owned a fifty-one percent share. Now it was Saturday morning of the Memorial Day weekend. Dee enjoyed the time she spent with Jared at their upstate New York home on Blue Hill Road, near Hudson. She had cooked breakfast, which they ate in the sunroom overlooking the valley.

"So, Jared, what are your plans for the day?" she asked as they sipped their coffee.

"It looks like I'll be closeted for most of it, my love," he answered. "First I need to chat with Barney and the crew to see about preparations for the Bermuda race. We need to have *Chauffeuse* in perfect condition and the crew prepared as well. Then I need to talk with Melanie and Mitch about what's going on at Protek. They specifically asked me to call in because some things are happening in DC that have them concerned."

Dee nodded; she knew these were the kinds of activities Jared thrived on. And she also knew it would give her some time to herself. She'd been eager to get into Hudson to poke around the art galleries on Warren Street. Maybe she'd give Em a call to see if she'd like to join her.

"That's fine, sweetie," she answered. "Maybe by three or four this afternoon we can take a break together. I'd love to go for a walk in the woods behind the house to see if I can find some of the old trails. Then a drink and dinner? Steaks on the barbecue and a salad?"

"Sounds good," he replied. "Let's see what we can get done on this beautiful Saturday."

Jared entered his office, which looked more like the space center at Cape Canaveral, and logged in to find out what was happening in this crazy world. He thought for a moment about the candidates' promises of more jobs and lower taxes. It was a midterm election year and it was the same old rhetoric from politicians who had never created a paying job in their lives.

"All talk and no action," he thought. "Maybe I should run for office someday."

Jared's cell phone buzzed. He looked down and was amazed to see the name on his caller ID: Joseph Benefacio.

Why would he be calling me? He's the one who owes me a favor. He thought about answering with Joseph's typical phrase, 'Talk,' but decided against it. "Yes?" he asked simply.

"I have a problem, and I think you might be the one to help."

Jared listened, remembering that some time back he had heard a similar statement from his government friend Stanley, which had led to his first encounter with Dee.

"The granddaughter of one of my neighbors disappeared three days ago on her way home from school. We have to assume she was kidnapped. I have put money out on the street, and my men have made inquiries, but nothing has come of it. This was not our doing, and I am at the very end of my wits. What do I tell her family?"

There was a long silence.

"Dominic will come up to talk to you; he will be our connection. He will use all of our resources to find the girl," Jared finally said.

"I will pay whatever you ask."

"We both understand what has happened here, Joseph. I cannot—no, I will not—accept any payment for this."

"Find the girl and return her to her mother and father. They are beside themselves!"

"We will do that, and the criminals will not go unpunished," said Jared.

"A lesson should be made."

"Yes."

The line went dead.

Jared looked at the phone in his hand. *Did I really say that? Yes, and I meant it.* He just didn't know who would pull the trigger.

His next call was to Melanie. The dice were rolling.

Dee still couldn't go into Hudson without thinking about the day, almost two years ago, when she was kidnapped. Well, almost kidnapped. It wasn't long after she'd met Jared, and she still hadn't known how much trouble her ex-husband Steve Milan had been in. Two thugs had tried to grab her as she walked through an alley. She and two of Jared's security guards, Mitch, and Mark, had nipped that in the bud, and Em, along with her husband Henry, had been the constables who had taken the bad guys to jail. Dee loved Em for her spunk and her spirit and loved her and her husband like family.

Em was thrilled to get Dee's phone call, and in half an hour, she was at her door. She knew her friend was in town, but didn't expect to see her unless they all went to the Memorial Day celebration in the park. Em was usually busy managing the Bed & Breakfast on the other side of the Hudson River, but today she was taking a few hours off to spend time with Dee.

"I've been studying up on the art world—reading about it on the Internet," she said as soon as she was buckled into her seat. "You can't believe what's going on. It's truly amazing." Dee smiled and nodded, but Em could see she was paying attention to her driving. She knew they didn't have a car in the city, so when Dee came upstate to Hudson, she had to look out for the farmers and their pickup trucks.

"So, what's new in the art world?" asked Dee, with a twinkle in her eye, once she was on the road.

"Well," said Em, ramping up, "there's an art forgery ring in Germany that's sold over two dozen fakes. One of them was bought by a big movie star here in the US. When he found out he'd been duped, he quickly sold it at a loss, but the worst of it was the embarrassment."

"Oh, my," came the response, "how interesting."

Em continued. "The losses were huge. Imagine what it must feel like to buy a painting for a couple million dollars only to find out it's a forgery—that it's worthless. And the forgers are master criminals, conning people out of their hard-earned money."

"Do the articles say where the forgers are located—I mean, geographically?"

"Germany, Spain, Italy... all over Europe. There's even a forger they found selling his paintings on the streets of New York. It all began because someone asked him if he could copy a Picasso. And he did such a good job that now he makes fakes for a living."

"There's a new one on me," said Dee, filing the information away for future use.

"Well, all I can say," Em went on, "is that it's a good thing you work with new artists, because if you worked with old masters, like Dali, Miro, and Picasso, you'd need to hire an art consultant to help you separate the real ones from the fakes." Em went on, half joking. "You know, someone like me."

Dee answered her ever so kindly, "You are so right, Em. What would I do without you?"

And for Em, the afternoon was all she'd hoped for. She got to spend time with the lady she loved like the daughter she never had. They browsed the Hudson galleries, chatted with the owners about buyers and trends—and yes, fakes and forgeries—and then had coffee and cake in the local teashop before calling it a day.

Jared was pleased to see that his wife was home. She popped her head into his office, all smiles, and began to ask about the day's events.

"So, is the world under control today?" she asked lightly.

Jared's worried face told the tale.

"Tell me," she said quietly.

He told her about Joseph's call and the kidnapping of Lucy.

"He called *you*?" she asked. "Why *you*?"

"Because he put all of his people on the street and they came up with nothing. He knows that it's gone way beyond Boston. He's "family" and he knows he can't work outside his territory, so he called me. He hates me because I was there when his son died, but he also respects me. He can look into my eyes and see who I am and I can do the same with him. We understand each other. He came to me with a problem and we will solve it."

Dee shuddered.

"You know that Melanie not only runs Protek, but she has her ear to the ground about everything that goes on in Washington. And some of it's pretty sordid stuff. I don't even know where her information comes from, and maybe it's better if I don't. Sometimes I think it comes from Dom because he can be a wild one. I've heard he's as comfortable underground as he is above ground." Jared chuckled when he realized he'd said something funny.

She nodded, and Jared continued.

"Melanie suspected that the kidnapping and selling of young girls had been going on for a long time, but she couldn't put her finger on the culprits. Besides, she didn't have an interested client, but now she does: Joseph. All of her Sherlocks are now on the hunt. Somebody just petted the wrong cobra," he said, using a phrase he heard had been coined about him.

He watched the expression on his wife's face turn steely. He knew exactly how she felt about anything regarding the subjugation of females.

"While you were out, I spoke with Melanie and Mitch at great length. Then I called my friend Stanley, who is putting his government ear to the ground. I haven't talked to Dom yet, but I plan to meet with him face-to-face as soon as I can. I need to watch Dom's eyes when I question him. It's my best—no, my only—clue, since the guy could lie to me all the way to Sunday if he thought it was best that I didn't know something."

Dee was silent for a few moments, and Jared watched as she sipped her drink. He knew she had something on her mind.

"I think we should pack up early and go to DC—you know, be there first thing Tuesday morning after the holiday so you can meet with everyone in person. You could talk to Stanley and do some planning with Melanie."

Jared nodded, so she continued. "If it looks like they can handle it, you can come back to New York with me. Otherwise,

I can go back to the city alone and you can go to Boston and talk to Dom."

Not liking to be separated from his wife for long, Jared hesitated. "I have to agree with you. I'll ask Melanie to send the corporate jet up here and we'll fly down late Monday. You know how much I like spending time here, but duty calls. I don't like the sound of this. It has all the makings of a very bad situation."

Dinner was a quiet affair. Jared knew that their world had been peaceful for a long time, so he was prepared for what the future would bring.

Little did he know that, once again, it would hit so close to home.

Chapter 4

What a Crew!

JARED BROUGHT *CHAUFFEUSE* INTO THE dock at Newport with his usual skill and efficiency. The crew had lowered main and staysail, and were doing a harbor furl on their respective booms and hardly noticed; after all, it was important to have a smart-looking ketch when the race to Bermuda was right around the corner. Barney smiled to himself when he realized the engine wasn't running. She was still under sail with only the jib and mizzen up as Jared eased her in, and she had just enough way on to snuggle in without a thump.

Damn, he thought for the thousandth time, *the skipper is really good.*

Scott, the bowman, took the dock lines and dropped to the pier to tie her down. Joe lowered the jib and Jared did the mizzen. Another practice day done. Barney looked around to make sure nothing was adrift. Satisfied, he headed aft. His full name was, of all things, Barney Rubble. On the day he was born, his dad had exhibited a strange sense of humor, naming him after the Flintstones cartoon character. But it suited him perfectly. After people met him, they only laughed once until they realized he had a sense of humor too. He was six foot three and two hundred and twenty-five lean and muscular pounds, which could, if necessary, be intimidating.

Joe Oxford, his partner, was similar in size, and between the two of them, they handled the halyards to hoist the sails and the sheets to trim them. Jared liked to tease them by introducing them as his "engine room." Joe was new on the boat this year because Barney's regular partner was somewhere out in the Indian Ocean on a race around the world. But Joe could "hand, reef, and steer" and had received Barney's seal of approval when the two of them brought *Chauffeuse* up from Norfolk to Newport.

Another new person on the crew was Brianna Sweeny. Jared had stolen her from his arch rival in this race; it hadn't been hard. Barney smiled. Brianna had grown tired of her captain's snide remarks about her chunky shape and boyish appearance. That, and trying to get her below for "a little fun." Barney's smile widened. She might not be the prettiest stamp in the collection, but she sure could trim the sails to get everything out of them. And she could sense a puff of wind a mile off. He and Joe would be relaxing on deck when she would suddenly say, "port winch," and one of them would have to be up and ready to grind while she eased or took in the sail. She was also hell on wheels when the spinnaker was flying.

Poor Scott, thought Barney, referring to the bowman, *he's only a hundred and forty-five pounds now, and by the time this race is over, she'll have worn him down to a hundred and ten.*

Scott Anderson was the bowman; he was five feet six inches tall and all acrobat. Everyone said he should be in Circe d'Soleil; he was that good. Absolutely nothing fazed him. Ask him to retrieve a halyard at the top of the mast in half a gale and he was your man. Jibe the spinnaker, which was no mean feat in a boat with a staysail, and he'd be out on the end of the pole in a heartbeat. Barney shook his head. *What a crew!*

Then there was Jared. He was the kind of leader they would follow to hell and back if he asked them. Barney had heard of some of his exploits and they were almost unbelievable. He'd shared a few beers with Mitch and Mark, and they had verified the tales. Now, he and Joe worked for Jared in a boatyard in Norfolk, trying to make it profitable, so technically they weren't getting paid for this race, which qualified them as amateurs in the Open Cruiser Division. But Jared kept them all gainfully employed in one or the other of his companies.

Not only was Jared the best sailor Barney had ever known, but he was a great businessman. He specialized in finding small companies that were in financial trouble, like the boatyard, investing in them, bringing in people like Joe and himself, and turning them around to make them profitable. Over the years, Jared had become rich doing this. Barney knew how much it cost to keep a 45-foot, fifty-year-old Herreshoff wooden ketch like *Chauffeuse* in pristine condition. Barney had to appreciate that, as well as the fact that Jared's distant ancestor had really known how to design fast yachts.

They had finished cleaning up when Barney noticed a beautiful woman walking down the pier headed toward them— it was Dee. She hugged them all and thanked them for being Jared's crew. "I wanted to come with you for the race, but my business is really too busy right now," she said, laughing.

"Great, no cook!" replied Barney. "That stuff Brianna feeds us tastes awful."

Brianna gave him a playful punch on the bicep, which was more like a sledgehammer blow.

"Ouch," said Barney, "that hurt!"

"Serves you right," she retorted. "I try to keep you gorillas alive and fueled up and this is the thanks I get?"

They started down the dock when another crew and skipper appeared. They stopped to look. When they saw who it was, Barney and Joe moved forward to stand next to Jared. They all knew each other. The sailing community was tight, especially among the best, but that didn't mean they were the best of friends. Jared had rejected some of those friendships for one reason or another.

"No," thought Barney, *"it's all attitude. I'm the first mate and I wouldn't want any of them in my crew. They all wanted to be on deck in Chauffeuse. Never going to happen."*

The standoff dragged on for a few moments until the other captain, Nick Krumenski, spoke. "Well, Jared, I see you've offered yourself up on the altar of defeat for another year."

"We'll see," said Jared, with a smile. Barney and the rest of the crew relaxed a little. They knew who could sail the better boat. They looked over at *My Effin Life* and noticed the little things that didn't go unnoticed on *Chauffeuse*, like peeling varnish and frayed lines not properly coiled. They collectively came to the same conclusion—the other boat looked like a tired old whore.

"A thousand dollars," said Nick, "that we beat you to Bermuda."

"Make it fifty thou," said Jared, watching Nick's growing hesitation. Probably stretching his resources a little too thin, he thought. He waited to see if Nick would back down.

"Done. Who's the bimbo?" Nick asked.

"I used to be your trimmer," said Brianna before anyone could respond.

"Bitch!" spat Nick.

"Right," answered Brianna. "You got that right!"

"I meant the other bimbo," said Nick. "She looks like she could be a hot little number in bed."

Jared's eyes hardened like flint.

"If you're referring to me," said Dee, putting her hand on Jared's shoulder, "I *am* good in bed. Ask my *husband!*"

Nick closed his mouth.

Barney took in the whole scenario. "Damn," he said again, "I've heard it said before and I didn't believe it, but this guy has just 'petted the cobra.'"

Chapter 5

The Lurker

MARY ROSE COULDN'T WIPE THE image of "Smiling Dee," as she had come to call her, from her mind. Smiling Dee was everywhere—in her dreams and in her waking hours. The woman was, in fact, everything she was not, and that was what was haunting her. Dee had friends, and she did not. Dee was pretty, and she was not. Dee had a man, and she did not. When she closed her eyes she saw the perfectly coiffed blonde waves in her hair, the porcelain skin, the trim figure in a classic suit and cream-colored silk blouse, and the manicured nails. Oh, the list went on and on until Mary Rose could focus on nothing else. When she looked at herself in the mirror, naked, she saw a smallish woman with a body toned from exercise, but not delicate like Dee—case in point, Dee was everything that she was not. She hated that. She hated Dee.

Her days in Boston were spent meeting with her father's old business partners and with some of the new people she was bringing on. The good news was that she was an excellent manager and the time she'd spent getting her MBA at Harvard had not been wasted. Her days of having to strong-arm people were almost over too. Considering that she dealt with mostly criminals, it was a pretty strong team. Maybe some of them didn't like each other, but they all did well by her. In fact, barring unforeseen circumstances, she could go on in pretty much the same way for the next thirty years, keeping her head down and raking in tons of cash, for her father—for the family business—and for herself, each and every month. Eventually, when her father died, it would all come to her. *So life should be good, right? Well, then, why was it so awful? So unfulfilling? She knew why. Because of Dee!*

Mary Rose was not a deep thinker. She had a highly developed analytical side that she used for business, but it did not extend to her personal life. There her emotions reigned supreme. Her Italian heritage had taught her that family was everything. And family meant, first and foremost, her immediate family. With her dear mother long gone and Jonathan dead at Jared's hands, as she saw it, it was only her father, old Joseph, left to be her family. And she was so good to him; even now when he was failing, she still showed him the respect that was his due.

Jonathan was another story. She had loved her little brother, but from the time they were teenagers she knew she was the strong one. She watched in silence as he gave in to his vices time and again, and she made no move to stop him. In high school, it was pot, and by the time he was in his twenties he was heavily into cocaine use. She watched as their father tried to make a man of him by bringing him into the family business, but she knew it was only a matter of time until her baby brother imploded. In fact, when it happened, she was there to help it along.

She didn't see anything wrong with giving her brother the coordinates of her father's dinner date with Jared, nor was she surprised at the outcome. Jonathan had tried to kill both their father and Jared. He hadn't thought it through; the fact that there were two bodyguards had escaped him. The fact that Jared might have lightning reflexes and take the gun from him eluded his train of thought. Finally, when Jared reached into her father's pocket to give him his heart medicine, Jonathan tried again, grabbing the gun from the table and pointing it at Joseph. He pulled the trigger but it didn't go off because Jared had set the safety on, but the action doomed Jonathan. The two bodyguards simultaneously shot and killed him. One of them, Dominic, was Joseph's employee; the other, Mark, owed his allegiance to Jared. The two had become friends and were now coworkers at Protek.

In the end, she respected Jared and understood that he was doing his job. As she saw it, he was merely another businessman like her father—and herself.

But Dee was another story entirely. Here Mary Rose's raw emotions took over completely. Dee had once been, by extension, part of her father's empire, because of her marriage to Steve, but now Steve was dead and Dee was married to Jared. By Mary Rose's thought process, if Dee hadn't once been married to Steve, maybe her brother would still be alive. That made Dee—what? The cause of all her trouble? All she knew was that her hatred was now focused on Dee. *It is time to bring Dee down. Smiling Dee needs to go down in a blaze of glory! But, how, how to do it?*

That was the thought that consumed her every waking hour and invaded her dreams.

On this particular day, Mary Rose happened to be in downtown Boston for a meeting. When it was over she hailed a cab and within a few short blocks, she found herself stuck in traffic. As the minutes passed, her frustration increased. She tossed a twenty-dollar bill at the driver and got out a few feet away from the bustling Quincy Marketplace, which was filled with tourists and happy locals. Dressed in her usual dark business suit and carrying a briefcase, at first she felt out of place. But, then, in a moment of "carpe diem," she decided to enjoy herself on this beautiful sunny day. Her first stop was for a drink at Cheers, which lifted her spirits. Then, as she walked around, she discovered the entertainer on his unicycle and joined that crowd for a few minutes. As she rounded the end of the building, she found herself in front of a street painter who had drawn quite a crowd of watchers. This tiny little lady of indeterminate age had a large canvas in front of her and was painting an exact copy of Van Gogh's "Sunflowers."

"Isn't she forging that painting?" she overheard someone ask.

"Not if she sells it as her own. Then it's not a forgery. It's simply a Wang copy. I have one in my house. She does beautiful work, doesn't she?"

The second customer nodded and agreed.

"See how she puts her mark in the corner? It's a little star with two rays coming out of it. That's to show it's her own work. As long as she's not trying to pass it off as a Van Gogh, she's not doing anything wrong."

"Hmmm, amazing. Never thought of that," came the response. Then the two ladies wandered off, leaving Mary Rose deep in thought as she watched the petite artist put the finishing touches on her latest masterpiece.

Things were humming at the Galleria D in New York. Helen, the gallery manager, was in the main salon introducing herself to a new client. Nearby, in her own office, Dee was deep in conversation with Melanie for their monthly security teleconference. Jared was still at Protek, and Dee was constantly amazed at how Melanie could multitask and compartmentalize so many clients and their problems. Shortly after she purchased the gallery, Jared had sent two of Melanie's best people to New York to set up the security system, and Dee had yet to find fault with it. She knew that Melanie usually previewed the highlights and then shared them with her. Mostly it was routine news, such as the occasional pilfering of supplies from the stock room, but then she heard Melanie's voice change suddenly.

"Dee, I'm not sure yet, but I think I'm on to something." She paused, and Dee's head snapped back to the screen. "Give me a little time to go back and review tapes from the last month or two, and I'll call you back in half an hour. Can you get Helen in the room with you when I come back on?"

"Of course," answered Dee. "Is anything wrong?"

"Could be, but if it is, I think—no, I hope—we may have nipped it in the bud, so to speak. I'll be right back to you, okay?"

Dee waited for Helen's client to leave and then called her into the office, leaving the trainee on the floor. Melanie was back online in record time, acknowledging Helen's presence, and then asking her to look at a series of screenshots.

"Recognize any of these people?"

Helen and Dee sat spellbound as a series of random women appeared onscreen, one by one—all of a similar size and age, but otherwise looking like completely different people.

Melanie shot back. "Well, if you don't, the facial recognition software *does*. All of these seemingly random, disguised women are Mary Rose Benefacio. Dom tipped off Mitch that the word on the street was that she was very interested in you, so I looked into it."

Dee was the first to respond. "Oh my God, Melanie, that is amazing! I have never seen her in person. Jared met her when he went to Boston, but I wasn't with him."

A deep sigh came from Helen, and she spoke under her breath. "Now it makes sense. Oh, Dee, I'm so sorry. I should have mentioned this to you before. I've seen her here in the gallery and even talked with her; I thought there was something strange about her. I meant to tell you about it, but I guess I never got around to it."

"Helen, it's okay, I think. Melanie, you think there's no harm done yet?"

Melanie came back in her usual clipped style. "I hope not. I'm going to review the tapes even further back. I want to get an idea of how often she visits—maybe see if there's a pattern.

Meanwhile, Helen, see if you can remember any more about Mary Rose—especially the kind of questions she's been asking."

Helen nodded, and Dee could see that her embarrassment had not lessened.

"Our lady is up to no good. You can count on that. Despite her fancy business school degree, she's still a common criminal from the north end of Boston. And we can be sure she's not sightseeing when she comes to New York to visit Galleria D."

"Thanks, Melanie. This has been quite an eye opener."

"You want me to fill Jared in, or will you?" Melanie asked.

"I will, and thanks, Melanie. Let's get back together in a couple of days to compare notes."

"I think I'll ask Dom to poke around Boston. He's up there right now on another case, which you already know about, and he has his nose to the ground like no one I've ever seen. If there's any gossip around the north end, he'll pick it up."

The video session went dead. Dee and Helen sat there and stared at each other.

Chapter 6

Getting Down to Business

DJ'S CELL PHONE RANG. HE normally didn't answer it because he was a secret telephobe—afraid to talk on the phone. He could correspond all day long by email when he had time to think about what he was going to say, but a live voice caused him to stammer and search for the right words, which terrified him. However, this particular ring was a bugle call, and the only one with that special ring was Melanie. He was up and out the door in an instant.

DJ was Jared and Melanie's golden boy, hero of the previous year's Black Friday penny scam takedown. Hacker turned Protek computer whiz, he was a very immature twenty-eight-year-old. He adored Melanie, who he saw as his rescuer and mother figure since she had protected him from criminal elements by moving him to Washington, DC and installing his entire apartment within Protek's walls. That had been more than a year ago, and DJ had no intention of ever leaving.

"DJ, I need you here right now!" was what he heard. He quickened his pace, wondering what he was in for this time. He stumbled into Melanie's office and slouched to attention. "Sit down," snapped Melanie. "You're not in trouble. We have a real problem on our hands."

He listened intently as she filled him in about the kidnapping of Lucy and the fact that Protek was not only committed to getting her back, but to finding the people who did it and cutting the head off the snake. He paled and sat up straighter.

"Yes, Mel, what do you need me to do?"

"I want you to use every talent you have. If you need more computers, ask me and you will get them. I want you to hack into the young girl trafficking network so we can find them and crush them like cockroaches."

DJ nodded.

"My next call is to Ellen and Irving. You will send them any information you get and all the raw data you find. They will perform the analysis so you can keep searching. You've worked with them before. Right now we have no clues, so start by seeing what you can find out."

Melanie's voice softened. "DJ, we all know you're the best we have. Now, I want to see the same amazing speed and talent I watched when you were taking down the penny scam. That's all I can ask of you." He almost cried. He hadn't realized how much this company—no, this family—cared about him.

"I'll try," he started to say, but then he changed his mind, straightened his shoulders and said with conviction, "I can do it."

"Thank you," said Melanie, "Now I have to call Las Vegas."

DJ left her office, his mind at warp seven. Tonight he was going to consume large quantities of pizza, tacos, and soda.

———

Ellen was putting their daughter to bed when Melanie called. Irving was looking on with pride and happiness at the two of them.

They had been thrown together when Jared hatched the plot to relieve Dee's ex-husband of most of his wealth in Las Vegas. They were both computer geeks, so they had that in common, but she was

Playboy-centerfold voluptuous and Irving was a gnome. He was short, overweight, and balding, but Ellen loved him with all her heart. Even though they had worked together at Protek before, it had taken the Las Vegas gig for them to discover how much in love they were. The cards were dealt from that moment, and they came up all Aces.

Irving took the call and put it on speaker. When Melanie explained what was going on, they both sat up. This could happen to their daughter! It took on a new dimension for them.

"What do you need us to do?" asked Ellen.

"I've tasked DJ with hacking into any and all human trafficking websites he can find. He'll give you the web addresses and I'd like you to follow up. Not to say that you two aren't good, but he's the best hacker we've got, and you are my best analysis team. Dig in and see what's there." There was silence for a moment while Ellen and Irving digested the news. Melanie waited, knowing they were thinking about what to do. There was quiet conversation in the background.

"OK," Ellen finally said, "Irving will work directly with DJ, but if anything pops up that gives me a clue as to where I can buy a teenage girl, I will be all over it. I need unlimited funds, a website that Irving will set up for me, and all the Protek muscle you can spare. This is the worst kind of crime imaginable, and it has to stop!"

"Granted," said Melanie.

The line went dead.

Ellen and Irving looked at each other. Their pay grades had just ratcheted up a notch. This was serious. Then they looked back at their daughter snuggled comfortably in her crib and realized exactly how serious it was.

Chapter 7

The Bermuda Race

J ARED HEARD THE DCS CHIME and rolled out of his berth automatically. DCS stood for Digital Selective Calling and was a required addition to all marine radios. It also had a red "panic button," and someone had pushed theirs. All masters, that is, captains, were required to give assistance to a vessel in distress. It wasn't only a race rule; it was the law of the sea.

As he headed forward to the electronics suite (wouldn't Horatio Hornblower have loved that?) he could sense that *Chauffeuse* was sailing easier and faster than when he had turned over the helm to Barney and Joe at 4 a.m. Last night's storm must have abated and they had shaken out some reefs. *Chauffeuse* was lively on the starboard tack and he could feel her take an occasional wave over her lee rail, but it wasn't anything to worry about. His crew knew their business. He checked the clock as he went through the galley—7:30 a.m. Oh well, he thought, I got almost four hours of sleep.

Brianna had beaten Jared to the radio. When he got there, she was already on top of it.

"Who is it?" he asked.

"*Harmony*," she said, referring to another sailboat in the race. "She hit some floating junk and sprung a plank. She's taking on water faster than she can pump it out. She's two miles behind us and a mile downwind." She gave Jared the GPS coordinates.

"Where's the Coast Guard?"

"Two hours out and coming at flank speed, but they issued an 'all vessels in the vicinity to give assistance' broadcast."

Jared thought for a moment; he didn't have a choice. "Okay, Brianna, let them know we're on our way. I'll be on deck. Roust Scott; we'll need all hands."

"Aye, aye, skipper," she said to his back as he headed to get his life jacket and harness.

When he got on deck, Barney and Joe knew something was up but not exactly what it was. Jared quickly explained the situation and then checked the binnacle.

"Prepare to tack! We're coming to a heading of 3-2-5." That was almost straight back to Newport.

He took the helm as Barney and Joe headed for the sheets. They tacked and then let the sails out to run back down to *Harmony*. Scott came on deck.

"Brianna says that *Effin* hasn't changed course and the bitch is a mile back and about a half mile downwind of us. She's been sagging off to leeward all night. She just doesn't point as high as *Chauffeuse*. *Effin* is closer than we are."

"And she's not responding to the distress call?"

"No, Skipper. Brianna has been trying to raise them, but they all seem to be asleep over there." Scott smiled; you never really got to sleep during this race. "You realize that if they keep going and we sail to the rescue, they'll beat us to Bermuda and you'll lose your fifty thousand dollars?"

"That's not what's important right now. You and Joe drag out our spare bilge pump. I know we have some jumper cables that we can use to jury rig it aboard *Harmony*. We might have to give them one of our batteries too. Then drag out our storm trysail and a lot of line. We don't have time to fother it, but if we can wrap it over the hole, we should be able to slow down the water. That's where you come in, Scott."

"I'll do my best, Captain." He and Joe headed off to perform their various tasks.

"He's the best," Jared said to Barney. "Take the wheel. Course is 3-2-5. I have some calls to make."

"To *Effin?*" asked Barney.

"No. He wouldn't take my call if I paid him. But there are some other folks who *will* talk to me."

They got there in time. Jared brought *Chauffeuse* up alongside and Scott leaped over onto *Harmony*. She was down by the bow and obviously taking on water. Jared, Barney, and Joe succeeded in securing her alongside and then went to work. Brianna took the wheel and they got the pump and storm staysail aboard. Jared rigged the pump while the rest of the crew, along with those from *Harmony*, managed to get the sail over the hole.

At last, there was more water going over the side than was coming in. By the time the Coast Guard arrived with a real pump, *Harmony* was safe. At the end of four hours, she was floating almost high and dry. Of course, there was no way *Chauffeuse* was going to win the race after losing a total of six hours, but before Jared cast off and headed to Bermuda, he had a short conversation with the Coast Guard captain.

The crew breathed a sigh of relief when the island of Bermuda appeared as a hump on the horizon. Three and a half hours later, they were in sight of St. David's lighthouse. Brianna came up on deck with the handheld GPS and a compass.

In a few minutes, she said quietly, "We just passed over the finish line, Skipper."

"Are you sure?" he teased her. There have been boats that completed the 635-mile race and didn't quite cross the finish line in their haste to avoid scraping their boats on the coral reefs.

Brianna took a sight with her compass. "Bearing to the

lighthouse is 2-9-2 magnetic," she said, making the correction for deviation in her head. "We're good."

"Hands to the sheets!" said Jared. "Let's get out to sea again and away from these damn reefs!"

So they did. Back up north again and then around the island, down the Dundonald Channel, and into the Royal Bermuda Yacht Club. Needless to say, Melanie had a berth waiting for them. Jared headed down the pier with his documentation to find the race committee representatives. They appeared to be busy talking to another captain, so he slowed down until he realized they were explaining something to the captain of the *Effin.* Jared looked back at *Chauffeuse,* caught Scott's eye and pointed at what was happening. Scott saw it and immediately headed aft to get the crew. They swiftly secured anything that could come loose and headed up the dock to stand next to Jared.

The head of the Committee was trying to explain to Nick that they had disqualified him for refusing to respond to the distress call. Nick was telling them that he'd never heard it. As Jared approached, one of Nick's crew said, "Yes, he did. And he told us to ignore it."

Nick turned on him. "You're fired! You'll never sail with me again!"

"I wouldn't anyway!"

Then, one by one, the rest of his crew came up and told the same story.

"None of you will ever sail in any offshore race again!" yelled Nick.

"Oh, yes they will," said a calm voice. "They're a good crew, better than you deserve, Nick. I will give them any references they need. After what you did in this race, nobody will believe you anyway. By the way, you still owe me fifty thousand dollars."

"Try and collect it!"

"My lawyer will, and he will make sure you give your crew

the bonus you must have promised them." He turned to the sailors looking at him. "Meanwhile, if you tell me what you were promised, I will personally advance it to you for your honesty."

"In addition," said the committee member, "there is a fine for your failure to respond, *and* you will be unable to participate in this competition ever again. I expect when the details become public, other racing committees will agree with our assessment of your fitness."

"The Coast Guard also has some questions you will find difficult to answer," said Jared. "They will be talking to you soon. Don't expect to keep your master's papers much longer. They take the unwritten law of the sea very seriously."

The committee member looked at a note his messenger had just delivered. "The Royal Yacht Club has requested that you remove your vessel from this dock within two hours. You are no longer welcome here. The harbor master will come within that time and direct you to a suitable anchorage." He folded the note and handed it to Nick.

"You bastard!" said Nick. "I'll kill you for this." But as soon as he said it, he knew he wouldn't even try.

Jared looked at him, his eyes hard. "Just out of curiosity, what made you challenge me and then not respond to the distress call when I was ahead of you? Was it that important for you to beat me?"

"Yes, damn you, it was!" said Nick. Then he turned and walked away down the pier, his head down.

Jared shook his head. The two crews looked at each other until Barney went forward and offered his hand to his opposite number. "Let's batten down and then go have a beer," he said. The other man nodded and the group became one as they headed toward their respective boats. Jared reached into his pocket and unobtrusively gave Barney a few hundred-dollar bills, which Barney miraculously made disappear.

"There'll be grog and wenches aplenty ashore tonight! Har, har!" he said in his best imitation of Long John Silver, which wasn't all that good, but they all laughed anyway.

The race committee members had been watching patiently. When the salt had finally settled on the deck, one of them said, "There is one more thing we'd like to tell you, Captain Herreshoff. First, I am proud to say that my grandfather and your great-uncle were close friends. But more important, even though two other vessels in your class finished before you, not including the one we just disqualified, after we adjusted the hours that you consumed in aiding *Harmony*, it appears that you have won the race in your division. The maxi yachts won overall, of course, as always, but I'm glad to see that such a beautifully maintained ketch sailed so well and will take home the trophy."

Dee's plane landed at L. F. Wade International Airport just as day was turning to dusk. The small jet taxied up to the private customs area, and she was whisked through in a matter of minutes. As she emerged from the building, she saw Jared waiting for her, and she ran into his arms as if it had been months, not days, since she'd last seen him.

The hired car quickly whisked them away from the airport. Dee had never been to Bermuda, so her eyes were darting back and forth trying to catch the last daylight images of island scenery before total darkness set in.

"We won't stop at *Chauffeuse* tonight," said Jared. "That's okay with you, isn't it?"

"That's fine with me, sweetie," she answered. "I'm just happy that this week is over and I can spend time with you. Tomorrow you can tell me everything that happened. Right now I want you to kiss me and tell me how much you love me."

"Done deal," said Jared, holding her even closer.

In less than half an hour, they pulled up in front of The Reefs Resort and Club, where Jared had reserved a suite. It was, in fact, their equivalent of the presidential suite, and was usually held in reserve for foreign dignitaries visiting the island. Tonight it would be theirs. Jared took Dee in his arms and kissed her lightly on the forehead and then on her lips. She responded with her heart and her body, showing him how much she had missed him.

What he didn't know was that not only had she missed him, she had actually worried about him during this race. It was the first time he'd raced *Chauffeuse* since their marriage, and she'd heard part of the story already. She was waiting for Jared to tell her the rest. But first, she wanted him, all of him, in her bed, with an urge so deep that she could not even describe her feelings. All she knew was that she didn't care about cocktails or dinner or conversation at that moment. She wanted her husband naked, in all his manly glory, making a woman of her. It was all she had thought about for the entire time Jared was away racing his beloved boat.

While Jared was still deciding where to place her suitcase, she was stripping off her clothes and unbuttoning his shirt. He lifted her off her feet as if she weighed nothing and carried her to the canopied king-sized bed. As Dee loved to do, she grabbed his backside and pulled him toward her, wiggling into his strong embrace. She couldn't get enough of him; his manly scent was her aphrodisiac.

"Jared, my love, I will never get enough of you as long as I live," she said to him just as she lost all rational thought and gave in totally to her senses. "Make love to me, my darling, like you've never done before."

Chapter 8

The Scheming Begins

O NCE AGAIN, MARY ROSE FOUND herself on her terrace on a steamy Friday night, drink in hand. She'd been to see old Joseph, as she'd taken to calling him, and now she was deep in thought, pondering a request he'd made earlier.

"You know," he had said, "I'm not getting any younger."

Mary Rose had nodded at the inevitability of that statement.

"I want you to go to Italy."

"What?"

"I have some things—some *family* things—I want you to take to my sister. I'd like you to get to know your aunt and your cousins. You know how I feel about family."

She nodded and watched as her father's head bobbed up and down as though he was trying to keep from dozing off.

"But the business?"

"It will run itself for a week. That's all the time you will need. Buy yourself a ticket for a Friday night later this summer and return a week later," he told her. "I will give you some gifts to bring to Italy, and you will go in my place. I am too old to see my country again. It's all in my memories now, Maria Rosa, using her birth name. You will go in my place."

Dutifully, she had kissed her father on the cheek and left the room as dusk was settling into the corners. She knew the housekeeper would come in soon to feed him some soup and put him to bed early.

What could possibly be so important that I have to waste my

35

time going to Italy? She was annoyed; in the past year and a half, she had become a creature of habit, which meant taking care of business in Boston and making the occasional trip to New York to spy on Dee. And now her father was asking her to drop everything to go to Italy so she could bring trinkets to family members she hadn't seen since she was thirteen. Why?

By her second drink, she was coming around to the idea. And midway through drink number three, she was mentally packing her bags and wondering if Italian men were as good in bed as everyone said they were. Make that Sicilian men, because that's where she'd be going.

She knew that if she was going to make the trip this summer, she would have to be sure her various businesses were running smoothly and that she had the people in place to take care of anything that needed attention while she was away.

On Monday morning, she called the travel agent and booked first-class seats on Alitalia.

Chapter 9

The Clues Add Up

ELANIE CALLED DJ INTO HER office. "Good morning, DJ. Have a seat. First, what have you found out about the missing girls?"

"There's a lot on the Internet, Mel, but most of it's about teenage girls who ran away from home or took off with their boyfriends. They either turn up and eventually go home, or they're found dead. Some of what I read would make you sick. There is vague talk about girls being sold into slavery, but we don't know where they're going. It's kind of a random noise sample. I did run some of the data by a math friend of mine who specializes in chaos theory to see if he could detect any kind of pattern under the surface."

Melanie mentally rolled her eyes, wondering who this person was and what he looked like. She wouldn't have guessed if she passed him on the street; his looks were the exact opposite of DJ's.

DJ continued. "Anyway, he did notice some patterns. When he applied correlation theory using known criminals in human trafficking from the FBI's files, which the FBI doesn't know we can access, he didn't come up with much. There are reasonable probabilities that the best-guess destination for the sale of young girls is Russia, followed a close second by the Middle East. Malaysia comes in a long third and China is a distant fourth, because they have their own sources. We need to keep digging, Mel, and fast. Let's set up a conference call right now and brainstorm this."

"Done," said Melanie. "Give me half an hour to set it up."

It's time to start putting the clues together, thought Jared. The videoconference Melanie organized included the Washington team as well as Ellen and Irving from Las Vegas.

Jared opened the session. "What have we know so far about human trafficking?"

DJ told them about the math professor's analysis.

"Interesting," said Irving. "Ellen has been combing through missing girl reports, and I found two who popped up briefly in Russia and then disappeared again. Not hard data, but, at least, a clue as to where they might be going."

"Anyone else have something to add?" asked Jared.

Ellen shook her head. "Nothing else that I've seen. No one is advertising young girls for sale."

"Unless it's coded," said DJ. "Maybe we should investigate this some more."

"Do it," said Jared.

He didn't waste time telling them how important it was or that time was of the essence. They already knew that.

"One thing occurs to me," said Jared. "How are the girls being smuggled out of the US? I think I might know someone who can give me that answer, and he owes me a favor. I'll take that action item to see what I can find out."

The meeting was adjourned.

Jared retired to his office and placed a call to Joseph. After the usual amenities, he brought him up to speed on what they found.

"My first question is, how are the girls getting out of the US? The second is, are they going to the Middle East or to Russia?

Dee's ex-husband had contacts I'm sure you know about, so if you could ask them discreetly about this, it would help us focus our investigation. Whatever information they can provide will be held in strict confidence, and there will be no repercussions for anyone who helps. You have my word on that. You and I, my friend, are working together to bring this girl back to her family."

Joseph thought for a few moments. "Yes," he said, "there is one person who might be able to help. I still do business with him, although it is much diminished since Dee's ex-husband's tragic demise."

Jared smiled thinly, knowing that Joseph had had him wrapped in chains and dropped into the Hudson River.

"Yes, I think this man will help us," said Joseph. "We do talk occasionally and he manages to import Iranian caviar for me and sometimes even Russian Beluga. I will call him. I think he will be most interested because he knows about you and has followed your exploits. He respects you greatly."

"Oh?" said Jared. "And why is that?"

"Because after you took Steve Milan for all he was worth, and then "acquired" his wife, he asked me if we should do something about you. I told him that if he liked petting cobras, he could be my guest. I'll call you as soon as he gets back to me."

When Joseph hung up, Jared looked at his phone and then laughed out loud. *So that's where that phrase came from!*

Chapter 10

DJ's on His Own

A FTER THE VIDEOCONFERENCE ENDED, MELANIE motioned for DJ to stay behind.

"DJ, you may have noticed how fast Protek is growing. Our once almost-bare building is now filled to capacity with new hires and new equipment. I think it's time you got your own apartment. I need the space, and there's no longer any need for you to be under our protection."

"Oh, no, Melanie! Please, no. I like it here."

"I know you do, DJ. But we are bursting at the seams and the one thousand square feet your place occupies will give me just enough cubes for the new social media department. Now here's what's going to happen."

She watched as his face fell and she thought for a moment he was going to cry. She tried to look benevolent.

"I have located an apartment building near here that looks very much like the place where you used to live in New Jersey. Six apartments; the two on the top floor will be made into one big one for you. I have purchased it with money from the paychecks you keep forgetting to cash, so it's free and clear in your name. The tenants don't know it yet, but their rent will be reduced to one dollar a year, payable to their favorite charity. This will be wonderful news for them because they are all on fixed incomes."

Melanie could see that DJ wanted to speak, so she quickly motioned for him to wait until she'd finished.

"Protek will cover utilities and repairs. I'm even getting the

40

elevator fixed. We're completely renovating the wiring so you can run your Cray prehistoric computer and heat the building with it. Oh, and remember your janitor friend from New Jersey? I found out he fell on hard times, so I'm bringing him down here to be the super. He gets the apartment in the basement. As for commuting, remember that big Harley in the motor pool that you've been drooling over? Well, it's yours. Any questions?"

Melanie watched as DJ's mind digested all of this.

"When do I meet my tenants?" he finally asked.

"Whenever you want to."

"I don't have a choice, do I?"

"You're still a member of our family, DJ—a very important member."

Call it the end of an era, she thought. DJ was a twenty-eight-year-old teenager, and it was not going to be an easy transition for him. He had grown professionally, but in his personal life, he was still a boy.

DJ sure hadn't seen that one coming. He loved his life in Washington. He loved working for Melanie. She was the best! He liked it when she brought her son Evan over in the afternoons for an hour or two. Evan was only a baby, but he was a cool kid. He would follow DJ into his apartment and climb onto the sofa, calling for DJ's kitties to come out so he could pet them. Once he had pulled their tails, so now they were wary of him and hid when they heard him coming. Yes, he was going to miss all that.

Now, feeling a bit hungry after all this mental exertion, DJ headed down the hall to the break room to see what was available in his favorite food groups—sodas and snack foods. If he were to be perfectly honest with himself, he wasn't hungry; he was "peckish," as his mother used to say.

And, there, like a vision of loveliness, thought DJ, standing in front of the huge vending machine, was the tiniest, prettiest girl he had ever seen. He was sure she wasn't even five feet tall and her hair was long, dark, and ever so silky. Her eyes were following up and down the rows of snacks behind the glass as if she'd never seen a vending machine before. So he stood there and admired her for a minute.

"Hi," he finally said. "Can I help you?" *Lame!* "I'm DJ. Who are you?"

"Hi," she replied, her eyes never leaving the rows of candies and snacks. "My name is Gloria."

Not used to exchanging pleasantries, especially with pretty young ladies, he waited for her to make her selection and then made his. He started to walk out the door, but at the last moment, he turned around and sat down at the break table across from Gloria.

"I've never seen you here before," he said.

"I know," she replied. "It's my first day. Melanie was going to show me around and introduce me as soon as she found the time, but she hasn't had a free second all morning."

DJ knew he was part of that problem, so he didn't answer right away.

"So, what do you do?" he asked.

"Social media research is what I do," she answered in an interesting accent that DJ could not quite place. "That's my specialty."

DJ didn't think she looked old enough to have a specialty, so he raised an eyebrow for her to continue. Then he realized that Melanie was moving *his home* to make room for this girl and her social media research department.

He didn't know whether to laugh or to cry.

Chapter 11

Dom Does Boston

A COUPLE OF WEEKS BACK, DOM *had sauntered into Melanie's office, wondering what kind of trouble he'd gotten himself into this time. But one look at her eyes had told him this was serious. And her voice—no, her bark—was tight, he remembered thinking to himself.*

"Something important has come up and Jared thinks you are the best person to handle it." She told him how Joseph had called Jared and told him about the kidnapping and what they were going to do about it. Dom almost exploded from his chair when he heard the girl's name. "Lucy!" he burst out. "I know her. I used to hang out with her father's younger brother. I know the whole family. They're like my own!"

Dom was shaking with rage as all of the implications of what he had heard came rushing together in his mind. "Let me find them, Melanie. Please! Let me be the one to find the kidnappers."

"Since you know Joseph, you'll be our main contact. Gather as much information as you can from his people and whomever you know on the street. Joseph has not been successful, so I'm hoping you will be," she continued. "Contact me every day through this cell phone," she said, handing it to him. "Irving and DJ will be given what you find out, and they will add it to whatever they discover. We're going to work very hard on this. I don't have to tell you that time is of the essence before the girl disappears forever. Here are your tickets to Boston. Do you need a gun?"

Dom said, "No, if I need one in Boston, I know where to find one on the street." Then he thought, we are really going after this. Melanie is pissed. She never calls them guns; it's always firearms.

"You have ninety minutes to make the plane," were the last words he heard as he ran out the door. Dom grabbed the duffle bag he kept in his office for times like this and headed for Reagan International.

When Dom got to Boston, he didn't have much luck with Joseph. First, his bullet was one of the two that killed Jonathan, the old man's son. Second, the muscle Joseph had put out on the street didn't know what to ask when looking for Lucy, so they came up with nothing. Joseph pulled a copy of the police report on the missing girl, but since it had been filed three days after she was gone, it was sparse—listing only her name, description, and her probable route home from school. Dom thanked him politely, noting the changes in the man that had occurred since he had worked for him.

"My God," he thought, "He doesn't look like he'll last out the year."

Dom made Joseph's muscle take him on the route from the school to her home. He thought of himself as a sniper looking for a good place to make a kill. It was the same thing as putting himself in the role of the kidnappers, trying to figure out the best place to grab her.

He came up with four locations, and then promptly ruled out three of them as being too conspicuous in neighborhoods on busy streets. He settled on the corner of the park. *Might as well start there*, he thought. The park was empty and the muscle couldn't give him any information about who might have been there, so he thanked them and headed to the police station. The muscle gave him a look that said, "If we hadn't been ordered to take you around, we would have broken your back." Dom smiled and gave them the same kind of look back, knowing he could take them in a heartbeat. They looked at each other and got the message.

At the police department, Dom ran straight into a bureaucracy roadblock. It felt like wading through mud. Finally, he called Melanie, and shortly thereafter, things began to change. He was approached by a lieutenant, whom, when Dom explained what he wanted, introduced him to a detective.

"I need to know all about this park," he said. "Who frequents it, what type of people, when they go there—anything you can tell me."

"Sei Italiano?" asked the detective.

"Sì, e so che la famiglia," replied Dom.

"I know them too. I thought you looked familiar. Are you going to find her?"

"Yes, and I'm going to *kill* the men who stole her."

"You shouldn't tell me that," said the detective, "but I've already forgotten it."

He thought for a few minutes with his eyes closed and then licked his lips. "At that time of day, when school lets out, there aren't many people in the park. Mothers have taken their young children home for a nap so they can start dinner. There are some old men who play chess, but that's on the other side of the park, so they wouldn't have seen anything even if they could lift their rheumy eyes from their boards. Occasionally, when the weather's good, there are some homeless men who come out in the afternoon."

"Was the weather good that day?"

The detective thought for a moment. "Yes, in fact, it was."

"Tell me about the homeless people."

"Well, I've never had to roust them, but the cops on the beat say they look like soldiers. Kind of like vets, you know?"

"I'm one myself," said Dom.

Dom noticed the detective's instant change of expression to one of respect.

"Thank you for your service," they both said at the same time.

They shook hands and Dom slowly walked out of the station.

Dom hit the streets in earnest now, quickly cutting it down to the homeless vets. He had contacts who told him where they stayed, and it didn't take him long to find them. Money spoke and so did pride. When he told the third group what he needed to know, one man stood up.

"Sir, you were an officer?"

"First Lieutenant. And you are?"

"Peters, sir. First Sergeant, Signal Corps."

"What can you tell me, Peters?"

"I think I saw it happen, sir. It was a nice day and I was relaxing in the park. I go there to watch the kids and think about what it would be like to have a life like that."

"Come with me, First Sergeant; I am going to take you back there and you will look around and tell me everything you saw, heard, or felt on that day."

"Yes, sir!" Peters saluted.

They stood at the corner of the park and Peters looked around. "I was over there, LT, sitting on the ground. Let me think. You know how you notice everything when you're in enemy territory? You never lose that."

"I know," said Dom quietly.

"Well, this black SUV drove up and parked, and I thought that was a funny thing to do, so I watched. Two men got out and wandered around the front of it. I thought they might be having engine trouble and were waiting for a tow truck. Then, this little girl came along and caught their attention. I swear, sir, it happened so fast; if I could have stopped it, I would have. I'm still in pretty good shape, but they grabbed her and slapped something across her face, threw her in the back seat, and then raced off."

"Did you hear them say anything?"

"Yes, sir, but I didn't understand it. My surname is Petersen and I'm Swedish. I speak and understand Swedish and Danish, and of course, French, German, Italian, British English, and American. Oh, and some Farsi, but it wasn't that either. I don't know what it was. It sounded maybe Eastern European."

"Привет, Товарищ," said Dom.

"Yes, that's what it sounded like. What does it mean?"

"Hello, comrade. It's the only phrase I know in Russian."

"Of course. I should have recognized it. They must have been Russian!"

"Da, tovarich, Russian," said Dom.

"So they will take her to Russia?"

"They will sell her to the highest bidder, and she will bring a high price. She's young, pretty, and a virgin," said Dom disgustedly.

"Can we find her?" asked Peters, but Dom was already on his cell to Melanie.

"We have a lead," said Dom. "No one else picked up on it but I found a guy who was actually there. They were Russians. They spoke Russian!"

There was a long silence at the other end. "Russian?" Melanie said quietly, "Well that ties it! Sight in your rifle, Dom; we now know where to start looking. You just painted a big red bull's-eye on someone's back."

"One more thing, Mel, the guy who gave me the lead is a three-tour homeless vet, and he's living on the street. Can we do something for him?"

A moment passed, and then Melanie said, "Hand him the phone. I want to talk to him."

Peters heard a command. "Name, rank, and serial number, soldier."

He automatically gave it without thinking.

"Don't go away, Peters."

Peters looked at the phone. "Who was that?" he asked.

"If I'm right, and you are clear and clean, she'll be your new boss. Right now, she's accessing classified files to pull up your packet. How come the VA couldn't get you a job?"

"Everyone's frightened about that post-combat thing. It's in my record that even though I was Signal Corps, I've been in my share of firefights and come out alive. Nobody wants to touch me. I have my associate's degree in computer science and I would have gotten my BS if I hadn't run out of money. So I enlisted, thinking I could finish when I got out, but it obviously didn't work that way. The VA couldn't even find me a job sweeping floors or flipping burgers. They said I was 'overqualified.' Talk about falling through the cracks," he said bitterly.

A few minutes passed in silence and then Dom's phone buzzed. It was Melanie. Dom put her on speaker so Peters could hear.

"Buy him a burner phone and get him to the Acela train station in thirty minutes. It's the fastest transport I could arrange. There will be a first-class ticket waiting for him. Give him a couple of hundred dollars so he can see what it feels like again and put it on your expense account. I'll have one of our drivers meet him at the station. He's clear so far and looks good. When his clearance is confirmed, he has a job and a place to live. I'll explain when you get back, but basically, he's going to be security for DJ, and he's also going to have a linguistics cube here. Tell him that."

"Thanks, Mel," was all Dom could think to say.

"Served his country and his country screwed him. It's the least we can do."

The phone went dead.

Peters looked at Dom with his mouth open. He couldn't believe what he had just heard.

Dom barked, "You heard the lady, sergeant. We have things to do and places to go. And you don't want to keep *that* lady waiting—ever!"

Peters shut his mouth, snapped to attention, and saluted again.

Jared's cell rang as he was headed for a meeting. The caller ID told him it was Joseph. He halted in midstride and went back to his own office. "Hello, my friend," he said, although it sounded strange to call the man who had considered having him murdered a friend.

Joseph came right to the point, which was unusual for him. He sounded distraught.

"I have heard from my associate in the Middle East. The girls are not going through there. Apparently they have a new source of supply for girls that are not only, shall we say, just as pretty, but not as expensive."

"Well, that eliminates one destination, so now we can focus on Russia. We have confirmation that the men who snatched her spoke Russian. Now we have to find out who has her and where she is before they have time to spirit her out of the US," said Jared.

"I think I can help you with that too. I called a caviar vendor who wants to get back into the Beluga business. You know that particular sturgeon is a protected species and the caviar is illegal in the US. So I asked him how he would get it in. He said it was simple: pay the money and they will put it in diplomatic pouches. Four or five kilos brings thirty to fifty thousand dollars on the black market. It's more profitable than heroin and not as harmful. Anyway, I pressed him a little further about whether this would work going the other way, and he said of course. All things go that way too. Including people? I asked. Yes, he said, certain diplomats always seem to have more 'friends' going back to the old country than came into the US with them."

Jared's face hardened. "Thank you for the information, Joseph. We'll get her back. You can count on that."

Jared was on his phone to Melanie as soon as the line went dead. Then he called Stanley.

Chapter 12

The Plot Thickens

D EE COULDN'T WAIT TO TELL Jared about Mary Rose. As soon as he came back from his trip to Washington, the words poured out of her before he finished climbing the half flight of stairs to the living room.

"Did you know that awful woman has been wearing disguises and popping into the gallery at least every month or two since I opened?"

Jared looked surprised, but Dee got the impression that the look was short of total sincerity.

"I've been meaning to say something," he began carefully, "and now seems to be as good a time as any."

"Go on," she said. "I could tell you weren't terribly surprised, so this is not coming out of the blue for you, is it?"

"Well, you know that Dom used to work for Joseph, and he keeps his ear to the ground whenever he goes to Boston, which is quite often these days. For quite a while he's been hearing rumors that Mary Rose is interested in you, and, in fact, she seems to be carrying on the family grudge, but in her own way." Then he stopped so this new information could sink in.

He continued. "You know we've always kept a guard on Galleria D, and I wouldn't have it any other way. If there had ever been any threat to your welfare, you know we'd have been able to take immediate action to protect you."

Dee didn't smile, but she acknowledged Jared with a nod and a "go on."

"For the past year and a half, it's been business as usual. Whenever she flew into New York she would stop by the gallery. Sometimes she'd walk in and talk to Helen, but she would stay away if she saw you were there. Sometimes she'd just hang out across the street and watch the goings-on for a while."

"And why didn't I ever hear anything about this—until now?"

She watched as Jared shifted slightly in his chair, an indication of his nervousness over the situation, and decided to give him a pass. She knew he loved her, and that he had her best interests at heart.

"I talked it over with my security team, and we were ready to bring you in on this if the pattern ever changed—and it just has, in the last day or two. Now," and he took a long pause, "we need to start formulating a plan because Mary Rose is apparently escalating her visits—and her activities."

"I'm ready," said Dee. "We've always known we're not safe from that family as long as any of them is still alive."

By this time, it was getting late, but Jared wasted no time in calling a strategy meeting to decide what to do about Mary Rose; everyone who could potentially contribute information was to be in Bart's New York law office at 2 p.m. the next day.

When everyone was assembled in the large conference room, Jared made the introductions. He presented Melanie since many in New York had only spoken to her on the phone. Baby Evan was now in day care, allowing her to get away from DC to attend the meeting. DJ was there because of his computer capabilities, as was Gloria, their newly acquired social media guru. Jared had flown Dom in from Boston on an early flight, and two of the gallery surveillance team were also in attendance. Helen, Dee's manager, was the last to arrive.

Jared brought them up to date. Facts. One Mary Rose Bene-facio, small-time mobster from Boston, had a long-standing grudge against Dee. For a year and a half, since the death of her brother, Jonathan, she has been observed as she made monthly visits to Galleria D, sometimes standing across the street, lurking, and sometimes coming inside to talk to Helen, but only when Dee wasn't there. She often wore some kind of disguise, but Melanie's facial recognition software had given her away, thus enabling the team to keep better track of her. So far there had been no particular pattern to her visits, and, based on their interview with Helen, neither had there been any specific direction to her questions—other than her demonstrated curiosity about Dee.

Then Jared motioned for Dom to come forward and tell them what had motivated the escalation. Dom, always quick and to the point, began immediately: "Seems as though Mary Rose has taken a sudden interest in *aht*," he told the group in his Boston accent, meaning *art*. "In the last couple of weeks, she has been to almost every major art gallery in the city, as well as to the Boston Museum of Art and the Isabella Stewart Gardner Museum. She doesn't spend a lot of time in any one place, but when she talks to people she comes outside and writes things down in a little notebook as if she wants to remember the important points."

Someone spoke up. "What kinds of art galleries, Dom?"

"Doesn't seem to matter. It looks like she wants to get a feel for the biz, maybe like she wants to buy one." Then he thought for a minute. "But that doesn't make sense. Why would she want an art gallery?"

Jared entered the conversation again. "Do you get the feeling she's planning something?"

"Too soon to tell, boss," said Dom, "but she wouldn't be spooking around galleries if she didn't have some kind of idea in her head. She's not one to waste time on something she thinks is unimportant. I wouldn't put it past her to be planning something against Dee. That's why we need to put a counterplan in place."

Melanie, who had been listening intently, spoke up. "It's not going to be easy to put a counterplan in place when we have no idea what her plan is." Jared nodded, as did a few others. She continued, "She could be going in any number of directions. I suggest, for a start, that we increase our surveillance. Perhaps we can get our people closer so they can overhear some of her conversations. Do we have any women available? They might not be as obvious as men—and one of them might even be able to chat her up in a ladies' room or something. What do you think?"

Mitch spoke up. "We have our first two women completing training this week. Jared?"

Jared nodded, liking the idea, and at the same time wondering how long it would take to implement this and weighing the possible benefits. Then he spoke up.

"We don't have a good track record with Mary Rose. She's volatile, and she's treacherous. She spends her days browbeating hardened criminals and thugs—and they respect her. She's one tough cookie. And we know she can sometimes act on pure emotion. I can say on good authority that she put her own brother in the line of fire, and I consider her responsible for his death. So, to say she's dangerous is an understatement. What I am trying to tell you is that she could strike—like a cobra—at any moment, and we need to be ready."

He looked around the room at his audience and saw they were all on the edge of their seats.

"Here's what I think. We put our plan in place to increase surveillance of her, but, if at any point, she simply shows up at the gallery and asks to talk to Dee, we let her speak her piece. It may be the only way we can find out what she intends to do."

Mary Rose hated Dee, and she knew instinctively that art was the key to bringing her down. She wasn't going to be a lowlife like her brother and try to kidnap her. She was going to formulate a legitimate plan to ruin her forever, and ruin her in the eyes of the people she loved most—her husband, her friends, and her clients.

She had the makings of a plan, but she needed to learn how to talk the talk and walk the walk as she had been taught in business school. She knew she had only one shot at this, and she had to get it right. Late at night, in her bed, she schemed and turned various plots around in her head. In all of them, she did something spectacular that ended Dee's career or made a fool of her or ruined her credibility—something that took the blasted smile off Dee's face—forever. But what? *What can I—just one person—do? It has to be something that will bring Dee down in a blaze of glory. No. What would be the opposite of a "blaze of glory?"*

Night after night, she fell asleep after hours of hateful thinking. But nothing gelled. Then one morning when she woke up, the dream stayed in her waking memory. She was back talking to the painter in Quincy Market, asking the painter to make her a fake. *A beautiful fake. A gorgeous fake. A masterful fake! And I will deliver that fake to Dee, and Dee will think it is the most beautiful painting in the world, and then, and then what? Buy it? No, that won't work.* But she did feel as though she'd made some progress.

So, Mary Rose began to visit galleries. She fit the visits in between her daily rounds of the business associates she dealt with on her father's behalf. She started simply, asking questions like the ones she'd learned in her Marketing 101 class at Harvard. Where did they get their paintings? What artists did they work with? Who were their customers? What did the customers like? How did you decide what a painting was worth? Why were some paintings so expensive? And on and on.

After a few weeks, she was becoming conversant with the terminology. She discovered there were different kinds of galleries, and they specialized in varying kinds of art. She decided—much to her own surprise—that she liked the Italian painters. Maybe it was her cultural heritage. She wasn't sure, but those were the paintings that appealed to her. She was drawn to the bright colors and the sense of movement, and she found herself wanting to acquire one or two that she liked for her new apartment. But, that was getting her way off track.

If her premise was to present herself at the gallery with a business proposal for Dee—one that could ruin her—what could it be? Still, no firm answer presented itself. The days turned into weeks, and still she fretted and stewed over her hatred of Dee.

Then, one night on the evening news, there was a story about how a painting that was stolen in World War II had been discovered in an attic in France and had been returned to its rightful owner. Now, when she heard a story about art, she paid attention and made a mental note of it. Now this was interesting.

That night, in the middle of the night, Mary Rose woke and sat straight up in her bed, a full-fledged plan spread out in front of her like a Cezanne fruit-bowl still life.

At last, she knew what she was going to do.

Chapter 13

DJ Comes of Age

ONCE AGAIN, DJ FOUND HIMSELF checking into a hotel as Melanie planned and executed the destruction, as he thought of it, of the only home he had ever known in Washington, DC—his "digs" inside the Protek building. He felt uneasy about this move; in fact, he was always uneasy when his life didn't follow a regular pattern. He even thought of the chaos of his apartment as a pattern. Despite his messy home, DJ liked order. He liked numbers and patterns and things he could count on to remain the same. And now, lots of things were changing, which left him feeling uneasy.

Besides being ousted from his apartment inside Protek, he was also having some strange feelings about Gloria, and he had no idea what to do about them. For one thing, every time he was near her, like when they were working together, he found himself inhaling the special fragrance of her hair and wanting to put his hand on her shoulder, but he wasn't ready to do it.

He took extra time in the morning, putting on deodorant, looking for a clean shirt, and searching for jeans that weren't all wrinkled, and, wonder of wonders—he had given up his beloved cigarettes—and this time it was for good. Several times Gloria had sniffed the air around him saying she thought she smelled smoke, and that was enough for DJ. He'd tossed his last pack away and vowed not to smoke anything—ever again. He knew that wasn't going to be easy, but he thought it would be worth it.

But, now that he'd done all that, what came next? He had no

idea how he was going to get from coworkers to "boyfriend and girlfriend," as he thought of it. He was twenty-eight years old and breaking ground that was the norm for high school boys. He decided to ask Melanie. She would know what to do. She was good about "feelings." DJ liked Melanie, but more than anything, he trusted her like a mother figure.

Little did he know that his opportunity would come even quicker than he expected, and not in a way he ever thought possible.

Later in the week, Melanie invited him to visit his new place. Technically, Protek owned the building, but Melanie had the two apartments on the third floor deeded in DJ's name, so they were his. She was in the process of merging them into one so he would have an apartment large enough to start enjoying his adult life in a comfortable setting.

Of course, she hadn't done this all by herself. She'd gotten the idea as she drove through that part of town one day, and then asked one of her assistants to look up the building with the "For Sale" sign on it. After that, she'd merely "organized, deputized, and supervised," as she was fond of quoting. Her dad used to say that, telling her it was the key to productivity.

As she drove the three miles to the brownstone, she filled DJ in. "There's parking in the back, so you don't need to worry about on-street parking. In DC, that's a big deal. And, there's a small covered spot next to the back door where you can park your new motorcycle. There's even a back entrance. I think you're going to like this place."

DJ's first thoughts about moving ran to the negative. He knew how hard it would be to get used to a new routine. No one would knock on his door in the morning and yell at him about a meeting in ten minutes. He would have to get up, get dressed, and get himself to work every day—in rainy weather or in snow. Now that he was thinking about it, the list was endless. He would have to shop for groceries, and he'd even have to feed his kitties and change their litter box.

Then his focus shifted and he dared to think about the good things this move could bring. For one, he would have a life away from work, and he would have his privacy. *If I want to wander around in my undies, I can. If I want to bring a girl into my place, I could.... uh, duh, yes, I could. Hmmm, this could get interesting.*

He let his mind wander in that direction as Melanie brought him in through the basement entrance. The first person he saw was his old super from New Jersey. The elderly man looked at him with tears in his eyes, and they shook hands. Then DJ and the old man hugged spontaneously. It was a totally new experience for DJ, and it left him with a warm feeling that he didn't quite understand.

Melanie then led him up the stairs to the first floor and then to the second, pointing out the nameplates on the apartment doors, telling him she would arrange for him to meet the occupants later. As they climbed the stairs to the third floor, DJ's level, he could hear the sound of saws and hammering. He felt, rather than saw, the first moment when Melanie opened the door. He had a sense of sunlight crossed with dust-filled sunbeams. Construction sounds and smells filled his ears. Not one inch of space was ready for occupancy yet, but despite the bare wood, there was a sense of *home* that surprised him. It was his—really his— and he could live his life here.

He had sixteen hundred square feet, twice the size of the downstairs apartments. Melanie showed him the open space and told him he could fill in the details. His head was swimming with the possibilities. *I can buy a large-screen smart TV and set up a high-tech home office. And what about a kitchen? Maybe I could even learn to cook.*

Melanie was still talking, but he had tuned her out. He was thinking about how he was going to get the key from Melanie so he could show Gloria his new home.

Gloria Patel was tiny, and her voice was soft, but she was a force to be reckoned with. An only child, she had been taught by two overachieving parents that she could attain anything in life with hard work, perseverance, and cunning. The "cunning" part came from her mother, who had used that tactic to win over her father, a well-established bachelor some twenty years her senior.

It didn't take Gloria long to come to a decision about DJ. In her mind, he had two very important qualities, the first of which was intelligence. Since her own IQ was in the genius range, she found it terribly dull to converse with less intelligent men, and she loved the way DJ's brain worked. She thought she could listen to him and never be bored as long as she lived. The second quality was her physical attraction to him, which surprised her since he wasn't her usual type. From the first day she met him in the break room she knew he felt it too. She recognized that he was a novice and she was tantalized by the thought that she would be his first sexual experience. Arguably, she would be the one with the expertise, but that didn't matter to her. Once she had set her sights on DJ, there was no turning back. He was the fly, and she was the spider with the silky, but very sticky web.

"So, DJ, how was your lunch hour?" she asked, sweetly.

"Oh, wow, Gloria, I don't know where to start. You know what's happening to my old apartment, right? I'm already staying in a hotel, and, well, you can hear the construction noises from here, right? Melanie is having my apartment demolished to make way for your social media team, you know. That's okay, I guess..." he said before his voice began to fade because he was afraid to hurt her feelings.

She nodded, trying to look serious.

"Well," DJ said, "Melanie just took me over to the new building to see my apartment, and it's just bare walls; I have no idea what to do with it. I've always moved into something that was ready to live in. How does it get from construction zone to I-can-sleep-there-tonight?"

Gloria's sudden burst of laughter filled the room.

"Oh, DJ, you've never done anything like this before, have you?"

She could see the befuddled look on his face.

"Come on," she cajoled, "after work we'll go over there—I'll drive—and you can show me around. I've done things like this before, and it's not nearly as bad as you might think. Why don't you let me *help* you?"

Three hours later, they were climbing the stairs, DJ, for the second time that day. Gloria had asked Melanie for the key, so this time, she was the one to unlock the door and usher him inside. The workers had left for the day and everything was quiet. Gloria decided to take her time. She had already told herself she had to be careful not to scare him off—and she suspected that DJ could scare easily. *Deep breath. Take it nice and easy.*

DJ's voice was echoing in the large open space. "So... where do the *rooms* go? There aren't even any rooms." He was pacing the floor, looking out of the windows, and stepping over construction materials and piles of tools.

As he stopped for a moment to look out over the tree-lined street, Gloria came over and stood next to him. "Look out the windows, DJ, and try to decide where you would like to be looking when you go to bed at night, when you work at your home desk, and when you have friends over. If it were me, I would like my bedroom to have a view of those trees, and from

61

my living room, I would like to look out onto the street to see who is coming."

"I get it," said DJ. "You're good at this, Gloria." Then he paced some more, and she followed him. "See these pipes—they are for the plumbing, so your kitchen and bathroom will need to line up with these." She pulled an agenda from her purse, selected a tiny black pen, and began to sketch a rough room design for him. "Like this, you see." He looked at her drawing, a four-by-six-inch miniature of his new flat. As he bent his head down for a closer look, Gloria moved in on him, knowing that this would be her best chance. Quietly she let her purse slip to the floor.

DJ was intoxicated by her exotic fragrance and the daintiness of her movements. But he was also exquisitely aware that this was the first time he had been alone with her. And now, she was so close to him that he was beside himself with joy—and with fear. Instinctively he softened his voice and began to curve his body closer to hers. He felt, rather than saw, her face coming closer to his. His arms came up and he wrapped them around her body. Contact!

Before he realized what was happening, he found himself locked in the most delicious embrace he could have imagined. It was heaven. All he could do was murmur, "Gloria, Gloria," while she swayed gently in his arms.

And even though she loved this moment of pure adoration—and victory—she knew she had to cut it short before she embarrassed him—or worse yet—scared him off.

"You will love it here, DJ," she said softly. "I know you will."

And with that, she pushed him away slowly and gently, gathered her purse and agenda, took his hand, and led him to the door.

As soon as they were back in her car, Gloria suggested they get a bite to eat, claiming she was in desperate need of sustenance. DJ, apparently still stunned by the embrace, agreed, just as she pulled into the parking lot of an Italian restaurant. She didn't realize it, but restaurant eating was also well outside of his comfort zone. Once they were seated, there was a moment of silence, and then they both began to speak at the same time.

"No, you first," said Gloria, "go ahead."

"I don't know what to order," DJ said simply.

"Why?" she responded, thinking he couldn't make up his mind.

"I don't know what any of these things are," he replied. "All I ever order is pizza, and that's takeout. Pepperoni and onion with extra cheese and a large cola."

At first, Gloria thought he was joking, and then she realized this was going to be one of those times when she would need to take control quietly without making him feel inadequate.

"How about you let me pick some things that I think you might like, then?"

He nodded, and she watched as a shy smile brightened his face, and he visibly relaxed.

"Good, let's do that, then, shall we?" And, with all of her experience, Gloria worked her magic to make DJ feel content and cared for as she called the waiter over and ordered them a delicious array of antipasto, entrees, and dessert.

———

Hours later, in his hotel room, DJ fell asleep thinking about Gloria's shiny hair, the way her laugh sounded like music, and how her hands felt that first moment she reached across the table to take hold of his. He thought that was a moment he would treasure as long as he lived.

As his tired head touched the pillow, his last thought was, "I have a girlfriend. At least, I think I have a girlfriend…"

Chapter 14

Change is in the Air

D J WALKED INTO THE MORNING briefing at twelve minutes after eight. He was greeted with smiles and grins as he took the seat next to Gloria—the one that had obviously been saved for him. For emphasis, she patted the chair seat and gave him a big smile. One of the new social media guys winked at him. *Guess the cat's out of the bag,* thought DJ. He was right.

At ten, Melanie called him into her office. "You wanted to speak to me, DJ?" she ventured.

"Yes, ma'am, I did, but thanks," he replied. "I think it's already been taken care of."

"Good to hear that, DJ."

He went back to his cube. Melanie was the only one with an office. Everyone else had cubes. DJ had recently graduated to a larger cube; this one had a table and four chairs in addition to his L-shaped desk and two work laptops. In the middle of the table sat a large book and several folders that hadn't been there the day before. He picked them up: fabric samples, carpet swatches, paint chips, and furniture catalogs. *Uh oh.* As he stopped to have a look, Gloria popped her head in the door.

"Ah, DJ, I see you've found everything."

He looked up and warmed to the now-familiar smile on her face.

"What's so neat about all these samples is that I downloaded a 3-D design program so you can visualize your entire apartment

on your laptop. All you have to do is pick out what you think
you'd like—like room color, carpet color, and couch print—and
I can put it all in the program, and voila, you will see exactly
what your room will look like. Isn't that exciting?"

DJ had no idea you could use computers to do something
like that. His first thought was that it would make things so
much easier to make his place livable. His second thought was,
what had Melanie done with his favorite ratty chair?

As if she was reading his mind, Gloria said, "Oh, and you
know your favorite ratty chair? Well, I saw Melanie telling the
workers to throw it out, so I asked her to save it. I told her
you were going to have it reupholstered for your new place. She
looked at me kind of funny, but she told me it would be at the
back with the trash until the recyclers come next week. So, we
better get a move on."

That clinched it for DJ. He knew he was under new
management, but he thought he was going to like it.

The days went by quickly, and soon two more sunny summer
weeks had passed. Gloria and DJ ate lunch together at the
table in his cube and visited the new digs after work. By night,
they tried out new restaurants. Gloria introduced him to Thai,
Cantonese, Indian, and Moroccan food. She took the time to
explain each culture's use of spices and seasonings and showed
him how to order a dish so that it was hot enough to enjoy, but
not too hot to digest. Since neither of them consumed alcohol,
they tried hot and iced teas, fruit juices, and sodas. As they
dined, they explored their own world of feelings, telling each
other about the meaningful events in their lives, as well as their
likes and dislikes, and even their hopes and dreams. The more
they talked, the more they found they had in common.

In a way, they were two lost souls. DJ, who had never known

his father, could only imagine what family life was like. Gloria knew and told him it wasn't all it was cracked up to be—that parents didn't really pay that much attention to their children anyway. They decided early on that their careers would come first, and if they were fortunate enough to have spare time and money, they would spend it traveling to interesting places around the world. Gloria had assured him that there were plenty of destinations he would love. Never having left the eastern seaboard, he took her at her word.

Meanwhile, they were gradually exploring more than just their thoughts, and DJ was the eager student, happily taking his cues from Gloria. They had not yet "slept over," as DJ called it, but they had enjoyed some romantic times together, either in his hotel room or in her studio apartment. As DJ's new flat, as she called it, rapidly took shape, so did their plan. They would have their first sleepover the day they moved in as a couple.

DJ was in a deep dreaming-of-Gloria sleep in his hotel room, when his phone rang in the middle of the night. It took several rings before he could turn off his fantasies and answer. It was his mathematician friend.

"Because of what you told me about the caviar, I made the assumption that it was a diplomat living in Washington and added that to my mathematical analysis model. There was an overall correlation of 16.879 percent with the Russians, but there is still a lot of noise in the data; however, statistically, it is significant. I definitely think you are onto something; I hope that I have been helpful. It's been a most interesting problem."

Chapter 15

Can They Solve the Mystery?

D J THOUGHT HE KNEW EVERYTHING there was to know about computers, but his world was about to become much larger. While he had been on the dark side for all these years, as he thought about the world of hackers and scammers, Gloria had become an expert on social media and social research. And, now, who better to show him and teach him than Gloria herself? DJ was eager to learn.

Today, they were going to combine their skills to come up with a profile of the man DJ had long ago code named "Iceman," since he was most likely the same figure he thought was the mastermind behind the penny scam. They needed a Russian language expert, so Melanie had found one. As it turned out, their linguist already lived in DJ's new building; he was a retired Russian engineer who came to the US to live with his daughter and his only grandchild. Always on the lookout for new talent, Melanie had vetted and enlisted him soon after she met him in the hallway.

"Today I am going to walk you through the basics of navigating the Internet's social media websites," said Gloria authoritatively. "You will need to know the basics of using Facebook, Twitter, Instagram, and LinkedIn, for starters."

DJ watched as her fingers flew over the keys, showing them sample profiles on each website.

She continued. "The search function can be an important

tool; you can use it whenever you need to, and it will give you additional valuable information."

She waited while they tried it out using their own examples.

"Now, let me show you how to navigate across websites and how to identify an individual and compare his personal and professional profiles."

DJ could see where she was going with this; he remembered the name of an old friend in New Jersey and showed Gloria how he found him on Facebook, LinkedIn, and Instagram, earning quick praise for his efforts.

"Now, let's see if we can find out anything about the Iceman," said Gloria.

DJ quickly realized how difficult their work was going to be, and since they were now going to be researching in Russian, the translator was a godsend. The trio pored over emails and posts that emanated from the US but were written in Russian. They were searching for keywords, like "teenage girl" and "virgin." DJ began to notice that in some of the emails a certain word kept popping up.

"Stop!" he told Gloria. "What is that word?" He pointed to it:

"I've seen that word before; it looks like "box" but, for some reason, I know it means something else. I'm not even sure how I *know* that."

The Russian translator stepped in. "It's like a term of endearment. It translates to"—and here he seemed to rack his brain—"like the Irish term 'boyo'—does that make any sense?"

DJ almost screamed it out. "Boyo! That's how the Iceman started out his emails to me. He didn't use my name; he called me Boyo. It has to be him. Who is he? If we can find out who he is, we have our man."

"It's him!" Gloria shouted as the last bits of information were translated. "We know who he is. He has some aliases and passports, but his real name is Gregorie Stepinkalie."

The excitement in the room was palpable. In a short time, they had his passport photo, his height and weight, his date of birth, his permanent address in Moscow, and the names of his siblings. Both his parents were deceased.

From the LinkedIn profile, they learned that he was a mid-level functionary at the Russian Embassy—the Public Information Officer. They got his work email address and a few of his business contacts. There were apparently no women or men in his personal life. He lived alone.

"Diplomatic immunity!" DJ almost shouted it. "That's why he's so bold. He thinks no one can catch him, and if they do, they can never prosecute him. He thinks he has us. Wait until Jared hears about this!"

DJ saw the look on Gloria's face and knew that her excitement at having found the Iceman was now crumbling in light of this new information. He put a protective arm around her shoulder.

"Can you run a report that tracks an individual's travel in and out of the US?" he asked.

"Of course," she replied, regaining her composure. Then, using the special access granted her as a member of a security team, she showed them how to set up the parameters and run the report. The 15-page dossier outlined trip after trip he had made from Moscow to several American cities, including New York, Boston, Washington, Newark, and Chicago. There was even one trip to San Francisco.

As soon as the electronic report downloaded, DJ emailed a copy to Ellen and Irving so they could cross-reference the Iceman's presence in the various US cities with the known disappearances of young girls.

Now in possession of a name, Gloria once again logged into social media.

"Stepinkalie doesn't have a Facebook account, but that's no surprise," she said. "He does have a Twitter account, and here's where it gets interesting. It looks like he has tried to hide his own identity, but he is following several subjects of interest—and none of them are good."

Gloria printed up a list of the people and groups the man followed, and at the same time downloaded the information. Then she sent it all to Irving and Ellen, asking them to identify the people, the groups, and the websites behind the online identities.

She turned to DJ. "I suspect that all of them—the Iceman and the groups he followed—were up to all kinds of evil."

Four hours of nonstop work and suddenly there was a collective sigh. "Wow," said DJ. "That was intense, Gloria. I had no idea you could find all of this information—and so quickly. You're amazing!"

Gloria looked up from her screen and gifted DJ with one of her huge smiles. "Thank you. I'm so happy to be able to help! I think he is an evil man and I hope we can stop him."

Then they both turned to their translator and thanked him for his hard work. "It was nothing," he said, showing his embarrassment.

They were about to close down the meeting when the phone rang. It was Ellen; they put her on speaker phone. "He's your man! We have an almost perfect match of the Iceman's travel schedule with the disappearance of teenage girls in our database. I'd say it's about a ninety percent correlation. Good enough for you? He could have sent an accomplice when he couldn't be there in person, don't you think?"

Gloria jumped out of her chair and let out a cheer, high-fiving DJ and the translator.

"We did it! We did it!" she whooped. "He's our man! There's absolutely no doubt that he's our man!"

Melanie, who was down the hall in her own office, heard the commotion and smiled.

Chapter 16

The Richest Man in New York

DEE STILL COULD NOT BELIEVE her ears. Klaus Vander Houten had just called and invited her to an "intimate cocktail party" to discuss art. She'd met him only a few times; he had stopped by the gallery once in a while, long ago, when she was still the manager, and she had seen very little of him since then. She knew him mostly by reputation—he was in his late seventies, single, somewhat of a recluse, and the owner of a magnificent art collection that included several European masters—all of it housed in an immense triplex penthouse located on the Upper East Side. She wondered who would be included in an "intimate cocktail party," never imagining what Klaus had in mind.

With Jared in Washington on business, Dee presented herself—alone—at the reception desk of Klaus's elegant old building and was asked to take his private elevator to the twentieth floor. Dressed in his tuxedo, Klaus himself answered the door, which surprised her, and he escorted her to a large open terrace where drinks and canapés had been laid out on a glass table. Her eyes took in the sweeping city view, and she thanked her host for inviting her, commenting on the gorgeous vista.

Much to her surprise, however, even though she had arrived half an hour late, she realized she was the first person there, and she remarked on that, not sure whether she should feel embarrassed about being there early.

Klaus led her to a patio chair and seated her. "My dear, I am so pleased you could join me for cocktails today. Perhaps you have not yet made the connection, but when I invited you to an 'intimate cocktail party' I meant just the two of us."

Dee's eyes opened wide as the implication of what Klaus said sunk in. Jared knew she was at a cocktail party, but—uncharacteristically—she had given him no further details, thinking there would be safety in numbers. Now there were no numbers; she was alone with a man she barely knew.

Klaus handed her a cocktail and began softly, "First, my dear, I want to congratulate you on taking over the ownership of Galleria D, and also on your marriage. And, yes, I am aware that you recently married Jared Herreshoff, and you both have my sincere best wishes. From what I have heard of him, he is a fine man—and you make a beautiful couple."

"Thank you, Klaus," said Dee. "I wasn't even aware that you knew anything about my career—or my marriage—so I am pleased to accept your congratulations for both."

He continued. "I have watched your career from the beginning, ever since you came to New York straight from college. I have a picture-perfect memory and can recall exactly what you looked like in the early days when you were a gofer for the old owner. I loved it when you came into your own and bought your first elegant business suit and stiletto heels, and sold your first really valuable work of art to a dear friend of mine. He still has it, by the way. He is another of your fans. You see, we don't have much on our minds when we grow old, so we enjoy the simple pleasures—like following the career of a beautiful woman."

Dee had been listening intently, still not sure whether to be flattered or alarmed. Then finally, she spoke.

"Klaus, ever since I first met you I thought of you as one of the art aristocrats of New York and have always been impressed by your knowledge and culture. It never occurred to me that you might be watching me as well."

Then, in one fluid motion, Klaus placed his drink on the table, stood up, and, in an intimate gesture, delicately tucked a loose lock of Dee's hair behind her ear.

"Come, my lovely Dee, I would like to show you my art collection."

An hour later, she had been through all of the rooms on the main floor of Klaus's triplex, the area he referred to as "the public rooms," although he rarely opened his home to anyone except his closest friends. She was starting to feel more comfortable alone in his presence; although, if she were forced to admit it, she did find herself on guard. Against what, though, she wasn't sure. Klaus was a complete gentleman, and he was treating her like a lady. She was amazed at the size and beauty of his art collection, which was composed almost in its entirety of portraits—most of them of beautiful women. Dee had lost count as they wove through the maze of elegantly furnished rooms that comprised the living room, the main dining room, a smaller dining room, the library, a music room, a study as well as several chambers that seemed to have no other purpose than to link the larger rooms and display even more art.

At the end of one hall, there was a private elevator, to which Klaus produced a key and invited Dee to step inside. Again the alarm bells went off in her head, and Klaus, seeing her hesitation, announced softly that they were about to see his most private collection.

Soft, indirect lighting gave the windowless room an eerie glow. Dee stood transfixed as she beheld seven of the most beautiful works of art she had ever seen. Without intending to, she gasped.

"Ah, my dear, I see I have your attention now."

Dee remained speechless, staring at the canvas at the far

end of the salon, which was surrounded by direct and indirect lighting that highlighted its ethereal beauty.

"I can see that she leaves you speechless, just as she does me, every time I see her. Is she not the loveliest lady?"

"Who, what is she, Klaus?" she finally asked. "She is nineteenth century and European, but why do I do not recognize her? Why do I not know this work?"

A chuckle escaped his lips. "She was painted by Antonio Botelli, and, as you can see, the artist must have been madly in love with her. It was well-known at the time that she was his muse."

"Of course," said Dee. "Botelli. His lines are so fluid, his colors clear, and the movements so sensual. But it is the artist's use of light that makes this painting so special—it appears to be almost translucent, doesn't it?"

Klaus nodded. "For his paying clients he was more conformist, but when he was in love, he painted out of pure passion, with no thought for the demands of his clients."

"Oh, there is so much more to it than that, Klaus." She stopped for a moment and then decided to ask him the one question that was on her mind. "How do you come to have this painting in your possession?"

"It is rightfully mine, my dear. Do not worry about this one, although if I were brought to task I might have trouble with the provenance of one or two of the other ladies in this room. But, this one is mine by birthright. The *Lady in Lace* is my great-grandfather's younger sister. While she was vacationing in Paris in the summer of 1888, the artist fell in love with her, painted her, and gifted her the canvas. Her name was Celeste. He was forty-six and she was twenty-four."

Dee could not take her eyes off the painting, and stood transfixed even as Klaus told her the story. In the back of her mind was the thought that this painting had to be worth well over two million dollars—maybe even three.

"There is only one photograph in existence. A very long time ago, in Luxembourg, my late father invited a journalist in to view his collection, and the writer brought along his photographer. This same article has been reprinted only a few times since then, and every once in a while some art critic raises the question, 'Where is the *Lady in Lace*?' Was she lost during the war? Was she stolen from a museum?"

"And all this time, she has been here..." Dee's voice trailed off.

Klaus sighed deeply. "Yes, here, with me."

Chapter 17

The Hot Boston Summer

T O SAY THAT MARY ROSE was busy was an understatement. With less than three weeks to go before her trip to Sicily, she was more like a whirling dervish! She had met with all of her business partners to make sure they knew what to do if something came up during her absence. The mere thought of delegating authority gave her a bad case of nerves, so this was not easy for her.

On top of that, her plan to ruin Smiling Dee was now in full swing, and her mental to-do list played like an old eight-track tape at the back of her brain. She had visited the art museums, but today was her long-planned trip to the main branch of the public library, located on Copley Square. The target of her research was the lost art of European masters, and she came prepared to stay a long time, take a lot of notes, and request copies of any documents she might need. And that included color photos. She knew already that she would have to wade through a great deal of information about paintings the Nazis stole from private collections and museums, and to familiarize herself with the great art heists of the past seventy-five years. All that she was prepared for; she was doing a master's in fine art—on her own—and in less than a month.

In the north end of Boston, Joseph paid a visit to the Castorini family. It had now been three weeks since Lucia's disappearance, and her parents were desperate for news of her. When he was shown into the formal living room by an aging servant, the parents sat huddled on the sofa looking more like shrunken dolls than a well-fed, middle-aged couple.

Joseph sat heavily, leaning on his cane for emphasis. Despite his frail appearance, his eyes were clear and bright, and, when he spoke, there was no waver in his voice. It was strong and soothing. "My friends, I have come to sit with you for a while, to try to give you hope. Please know that you cannot give up. The girl will be found."

Lucia's mother sobbed louder than before. "My baby, my baby girl," she wailed. "They took my baby."

Joseph directed his attention to her father. "I had my best people working on finding her. They did what they could, but they cannot go much outside of Boston, where I can guarantee their protection."

The father looked up, waiting for more.

"I have enlisted the help of an unlikely ally whose reach goes way beyond mine. He is an honest man and is doing this because he knows this is the worst kind of crime imaginable. If it is humanly possible to find Lucia alive—and return her to you—this man will do it. You have my word."

The man patted his wife's knee, telling her softly that everything would be all right. She never looked up and never stopped weeping.

Joseph pulled himself up with the help of his cane and was escorted from the room. As he descended the front steps, several schoolchildren—friends of Lucia's—were approaching the front door, talking in hushed tones.

In the solitude of his study, Joseph removed a tiny prayer book from a hidden shelf in his desk. It had belonged to his wife, gone now almost eighteen years, and he had always kept it close to him because it reminded him of her. But now, it had one final journey to make and one final task to accomplish. He took a sheet of cream-colored vellum, penned a few lines on it, folded it twice, and placed it inside the back cover of the book of verses. Then, deftly, he wrapped it in flowered paper, taping it securely. When he next saw Mary Rose, he would give it into his daughter's hands.

Little does she know, he thought. *Little does she know.*

At the local police precinct, there was a quiet meeting going on in the desk sergeant's cubicle. It was short and to the point.

"The case of Lucia Castorini's disappearance is going inactive. I'm reassigning the two of you as of now. I don't have the resources to look for runaways."

"Yes, Sergeant," they answered in unison.

Chapter 18

Mary Rose Makes Her Move

I T WAS A HOT SUMMER day in New York City, and, at Galleria D, everyone was feeling the effects of the heat and the never-ending parade of tourists, the ones they called the "tire kickers." What kept Dee going was the same thought that kept every city dweller going through the sweltering summer months—the hope of getting away on the weekend. For New Yorkers, it didn't matter where "away" was—it could be the Hamptons, the Catskills, or the Shore. The Friday night exodus from Manhattan was epic, and shortly she and Jared would be caught up in it—on their way to Hudson.

Even the tourists seemed to have dried up this late Friday afternoon at the end of July. They were probably back at their hotels, nursing tired feet, and deciding where to eat dinner. Dee was in her office, and Helen was only a few feet away, at her desk in the main showroom, when the unthinkable happened: Mary Rose pulled open the glass front door of the gallery and walked in looking like she owned the place. All Dee heard was Helen's sharp intake of breath, and a shaky "May I help you?"

Dee was on her feet in an instant.

Although Dee had viewed Protek's security tapes over and over again, she was still unprepared for the imposing presence of Mary Rose. Short in stature, with a swarthy complexion and dark, short-cropped hair, the woman gave off an aura of strength that was palpable. It was as though a large, formidable prizefighter had been constrained inside this diminutive woman.

Dee extended her hand, smiling. "Welcome, I'm Dee, the gallery's owner. How may I help you?" Mary Rose shook her extended hand and introduced herself.

"Pleased to make your acquaintance. My name is Mary Bennett, and I'm an art dealer," she said, handing her an elegant, embossed business card.

Dee led her to a Regency desk and two chairs, designed for receiving important customers, and motioned for her to sit down. "Thank you for coming. Now, please tell me why you chose to visit me today."

Knowing that she needed to listen carefully for clues to the woman's plan, Dee sat silently as her visitor began what was obviously a carefully rehearsed presentation of her work as an art dealer specializing in the search for lost and stolen paintings in Europe.

"So what brings you to New York and to my gallery? I see that your office is in Boston," said Dee, trying to draw Mary Rose out. Dee knew that she had to use all of her communication skills to get the woman to show her hand.

Mary Rose was boasting now. "I am expanding my customer base now that I have successfully built up my European contacts," she said, knowing that she had none.

Then Dee asked her, "And what of paintings that have not been seen since before the war? Do you have contacts for finding those as well?"

Emboldened by Dee's line of questioning and not even noticing that she hadn't been asked for specifics, Mary Rose continued along in the same vein. "I have learned to track down every lead. We have found paintings in attics and in basements, in the back rooms of galleries, and even in the storerooms of churches," she bragged. "Often we go to the small towns and ask who has recently died, and we see if their children have any paintings to sell."

Then, going way out on a limb, Mary Rose credited herself with several "finds" that had been made by others, finds that she had read about at the library.

This was going far better than she'd planned, thought Mary Rose, seeing that she had Dee's full attention.

"I am leaving for Italy in a few weeks, and I thought that perhaps a successful art dealer such as yourself would need my help finding important works for your gallery."

She watched as Dee sat thoughtfully and waited for her answer. "While I admire the great masters, I do not deal with anything nearly as grand in my day-to-day business. As you know, the prices the old masters command today are often in the hundreds of thousands of dollars—and even well into the millions. Most of the artists I represent are relative newcomers, and while they may become great masters in a century or two, today they are struggling young artists hoping to gain a foothold in New York City's brutally competitive art market."

Mary Rose was unprepared for this kind of answer. In all of her research, she had never bothered to find out what kind of paintings Dee exhibited in her own gallery. Her plan was suddenly in danger of going down the tubes, and her brain was working overtime trying to find a solution—and then Dee handed it to her on a platter.

"Now, I do have a few clients who collect European masters. They are extremely wealthy and very knowledgeable about art. Would you like me to ask around to see if there are any artists or paintings they would like 'us' to look for?" suggested Dee.

"But, of course; that would be perfect," Mary Rose replied, trying to emulate Dee's mode of speech. She watched as Dee fingered her elegant business card.

"Let me call a few of my oldest and dearest friends," said

Dee, smiling sweetly, "and I will call you before you leave for Europe. When would that be?"

Mary Rose gave her a date, stood up, shook hands, and walked sedately out of the gallery, wanting to shout for joy at her success, but curbing her enthusiasm until she was well out of earshot.

Helen emerged from the storeroom, where she had been hiding ever since the woman's entrance. "So that is her plan? Her big plan? Find you a painting in Europe and sell it to you? Why, that horrible woman hardly ever leaves Boston. She's nothing but a thug! How is she going to find you a European master?"

"She's not going to," answered Dee. "But she's finally tipped her hand. Now, I suspect I know what her plan is, and I also think I know what to do about it. Now, come into my office. We have some calls to make and lots of work to do."

Chapter 19

The Counter Plot

HALF AN HOUR LATER, EVEN though it was now almost 5 p.m. on Friday afternoon, Dee called Melanie and asked her to set up a videoconference that included anyone who might be able to contribute information and ideas. Within minutes, it was set up, and Dee watched her monitor as various people logged on. It seemed that Jared chose that moment to walk in the front door of the gallery, and Dee was overjoyed to see him. "Trip's been postponed for an hour while we sort out a few things, okay?"

"Of course," he answered. "What's happening?"

"I guess you'll have to wait for the videoconference to begin," she quipped as she sat down at her desk and turned on the security monitor.

"Good afternoon, team. Thanks for joining us at the last minute. Before we proceed with the meeting, I would like all of you to watch this short video of Mary Rose's visit to Galleria D just an hour ago. Then I will open it up for a brainstorming session—first, what you think she intends to do—and second, what countermeasures you think we should put in place."

No longer the grainy images of old, the video showed a well-dressed young woman entering the gallery and captured every word of the exchange between the two women. When it was over, exactly seven and a half minutes later, Dee heard various exclamations from the attendees.

"Now she's tipped her hand," said one.

"'Bout time; she's kept us in the dark long enough..."

"Wow, good show, Mary Rose."

"Okay," said Dee. "Question one, what's she up to?"

"She's not going to find you a painting; she'll steal one and try to sell it to you," said the first.

"She's casing the joint, and then her thugs are gonna rob the gallery," said another.

"It's a scam," said someone else.

"Elaborate on that, please," responded Dee. And so it went on for fifteen or twenty minutes, but they were starting to get off point, so she tried another tack. "Who's on from my Boston surveillance team right now?" Three people chimed in: two of her regulars and the newly trained young lady.

"Where has she been?" asked Dee.

The guys pulled out their notebooks and recited lists of visits to business associates: three trips to the public library, two trips to museums, and two visits to a local high-end print shop.

"Probably the elegant business cards," noted Dee.

Then the young woman spoke for the first time. "Dee, maybe it's not as important because Mary Rose only does this on her lunch hour; but, she's going more often to Quincy Market, which is quite a bit out of the way for her, don't you think?"

"I think you're right," said Dee.

"Several times she's stopped to watch an artist at work. She mingles in with the crowd and observes her, sometimes for quite a long time."

Dee said softly, "Please go back to Quincy Market and find out everything you can about that artist. And thank you. Very good call. Melanie, take note—that was a really good call."

Melanie started to wind things up, thanking everyone for their time and wishing them a good weekend. Soon, only Melanie, Jared, and Dee were left on the call.

"Well?" asked Dee. "What do you think?"

Jared was beaming, and so was Melanie.

"Bingo!" they said in unison.

Chapter 20

A Most Unlikely Favor

O NCE AGAIN, DEE WAS BEING admitted to Klaus's apartment, but this time, she had initiated the request with a phone call asking simply if she could speak to him. Klaus wondered what she wanted, but it didn't really matter to him. He was just pleased that he would see her so soon again. The matter at hand would reveal itself in due course, he thought, with the patience that comes with advanced years.

"You look lovely, as usual," he heard himself say as he ushered her into the front hall. He'd always admired her taste in clothes, and today's pale pink designer suit was no exception. "Would you like some coffee, my dear? It's that time of day, isn't it? Coffee, or perhaps tea and biscuits, as the English seem to prefer?"

"Tea, I think," said Dee, "with our chat, if that is okay with you."

"I asked the maid to prepare it before she left, so please join me in the private dining room." Dee did as she was asked, and soon the two were seated comfortably, sipping their tea. Klaus could tell right away that Dee was unsure of herself, and he was looking for ways to help her out when she finally began to speak.

"Klaus, I have a huge favor to ask of you. Moreover, there is no reason on earth why I could ever expect you to want to—or agree to—help me. It is far more than I deserve, and I am embarrassed to even think along this line. In fact, I wouldn't—if I knew there was any other way, but I don't." She lapsed into silence.

"Why don't you just start at the beginning?" he suggested.

"Oh, my," she answered, "well, let me try."

He waited several long moments, watching as Dee tried to compose herself, and she finally began.

"You know, I have always loved art, ever since I was in high school. It was all that I ever wanted to do. I think I was good when I first worked in the gallery, and later, I loved becoming the manager and getting to know all of you. You and your friends—the collectors of fine art—meant the most to me. I treasure that time and the relationships I formed along the way."

Klaus's nod signaled his agreement. "Go on."

"One of the things I was proudest of was my reputation. I was known all over the city as an honest and intelligent woman, one who was fair in all her dealings. I knew that my customers trusted me implicitly."

"Without a doubt, my dear. We all felt that way; in fact, we still do."

He watched as Dee continued, lowering her voice. "Along the way, I lost my way. I married Steve Milan, and I sold out. I sold out because I was poor and I was tired and I was lonely. I thought I could justify my decision somehow, but I never could. My life got worse, not better, even though I could finally have the material things that were lacking in my life. And, finally, not only was I lost, I was also in grave danger."

At this statement, Klaus looked up, alert to every nuance.

"Jared saved me. I owe him my life."

Klaus wanted to hear every word, every detail of this story, but he composed himself, resigned to letting Dee tell her story in her own way. It had to be in her own words, without interruption. He had heard the gossips, but this was far better.

"The man Jared saved me from, my second husband, Steve, was evil, pure evil, and so were the people he did business with. Jared and I believed that once Steve was dead, our problems with his business associates would end. But they did not; instead, they have now escalated. And, once again, I find myself the target of their wrath."

Klaus shifted uneasily in his chair, wondering where all of this was leading and how he fit in.

"The 'players' in this game I refer to are members of an Italian 'famiglia' from Boston. The father—who was once Steve's protector—is now in semi-retirement since his only son, Jonathan was killed. Jared was there when it happened, and I think old Joseph blames him for his son's death."

Again, Klaus waited for Dee to continue.

"His daughter, who is named Mary Rose, has apparently vowed to carry on the family vendetta. It has taken her a year and a half, but I believe she has finally decided how to take her revenge on me. She intends to ruin me, Klaus, to ruin my reputation in the art world and bring down the thing I hold dearest in my life—after my husband—my professional reputation. She knows that if she can carry this off, I will never work again, and my clients and friends in the art world will lose all respect for me—and abandon me."

As she finished, a huge rush of air escaped her, almost as if she were a deflating balloon.

"But, how?" he asked, after giving her a moment to compose herself.

Dee continued, giving Klaus a detailed description of what she believed to be Mary Rose's plan. Suddenly, Klaus was on the edge of his seat, nodding and even starting to smile as she unfolded her storyline. This was the most interesting visit—and visitor—he had had in years.

And then she stopped, he thought, for effect. "It would mean, Klaus, that you would have to go public with the *Lady in Lace*. Could you do that? Would you be willing to bring her out into the open? Show her to the world? It could mean a lot of publicity—and you have kept the *Lady* hidden for such a long time."

Klaus was silent for a moment, and then he smiled, a broad smile that lit up his entire face, making his eyes sparkle. "For you, my dear, I would do anything. I think you know that, my darling...my love."

Chapter 21

Planning for Lucy

J ARED CALLED MITCH. "I NEED you back on the line, my friend. I'll tell you why at the meeting tomorrow. Bring Mark with you if you can find him; you two are the best team at Protek. And don't say anything to Melanie."

"Will do," said Mitch, wondering what was coming down, but having a pretty good idea. This had to be about the Lucy kidnapping and he was being 'taken off the bench' to be in on it. Now that he was a father, he had no compunction about pulling the trigger on someone who trafficked in young girls. His next call was to Mark. After he explained what was happening, Mark said, "I've missed working with you, bro; this solo stuff is a drag. I'll be on the 5 p.m. into DC."

In his brief time at Protek, Peters had heard tales of Mitch and Mark that he could hardly believe; their exploits were legendary. He was just starting the workout regimen that this inner group did regularly, and he couldn't believe how tough it was. One of the women in the gym asked him if he was new here. "Yes," he said, "but how did you know?"

"Because they are taking it easy on you," she replied. "Wait until you start to get into shape." Peters paled. *What have I fallen into? Oh well, it sure is a lot better than sleeping on the street in Boston.*

Dom had silently come up behind him. Peters didn't know

he was there, didn't even sense his presence, but Dom had put his hand on his shoulder and said quietly, "We need you now. Follow me."

Jared opened the meeting. "This is about the kidnapping and sale of Lucia Castorini, known to her friends as Lucy. DJ, Irving, Ellen, and Gloria have identified the kidnapper. They have also hacked into his network, and we now know that she is up for bid on the international market. The current price is one hundred fifty thousand dollars, but the Iceman is holding out for two hundred fifty thousand; after all, she is young, beautiful, and a virgin."

He paused to let this sink in.

"What we are going to do is against the law. If you have a problem with that, you are free to leave now. One or more of you could be indicted for first-degree murder. The others could be implicated. Is that perfectly clear?"

Four sets of eyes looked steadily at him. No one moved.

Jared continued, "DJ has known of this the man since his hacker days. He is called 'the Iceman.' And he is just that: cold as ice and hard as steel. His real name is Gregorie Ivanovich Stepinkalie. He is the Information Officer at the Russian Embassy, and, therefore, has diplomatic immunity. There is no way our courts will ever be able to bring him to trial. But, given the information we have found out about him, he is not a 'person of interest.' He is not an 'alleged suspect.' He *is* the guilty party!"

The men's eyes hardened further; they knew what they were going to be tasked to do, and they were willing to do it.

"We have two objectives. We have located the penthouse where Lucy is being held captive; it's the Iceman's private residence, and it's crawling with guards. First, we have to get her out the building and to safety. Second, we're going to make a definitive statement to the people who commit this heinous crime. We want to make sure they get the message, 'don't pet the cobra.'"

Jared's audience was silent.

"Now, one last time. Mitch, does Melanie know about this? Do you want out?" asked Jared.

"Yes," said Mitch, "she knows everything; she reads your mind and my mind like a book. Last night, before we fell asleep, she rolled over, gave me a hug, and said, 'Yes, do it. It's the right thing to do.' I hadn't even talked to her about it."

"I don't know if they talked to each other, but Dee said the same thing to me last night," Jared replied. The other three men in the room listened, amazed, wondering if they would ever have the kind of relationships Jared and Mitch had.

"Okay, here's how we're going to make this happen," said Jared. "I'll be driving the limo that takes you there and picks you up." The others looked at each other, realizing he was going to be in as deep as they were. No one said a word.

"Melanie and her crew have been monitoring this criminal's habits for the last few days. DJ's been reading his emails for the same amount of time. He owns the building where Lucy is being held. Tomorrow is Friday, and that is the day he takes her up to the penthouse swimming pool when he comes home from the embassy. He always has two guards with him. We know that tomorrow the final bids are due, so he will be there. He's a bit of an exhibitionist and likes to parade around naked with her. His guards must be eunuchs because they ignore them. Either that or they know which end of the bottle their vodka comes from."

There were hard smiles from the group. Jared went on to explain that there were two security guards on the first floor, reporting in at fifteen-minute intervals, so they had to be hit right after they called in. That would be Mitch and Mark's job.

They would go in with plastic Glocks, which would get them through the metal detectors. Then they would take out the guards manually, with no shots being fired at that point.

Mitch and Mark looked at each other. "*Piece of cake*," their eyes said.

"Mitch and Mark will get into the elevator and strip down to their swim trunks. The elevator ends at the tenth floor. They will lock the elevator and leave their clothing in it so they can dress after they have rescued Lucy. We have the code for the elevator that goes the final two stories to the penthouse, but I prefer that we use the stairs. There will be two more guards at the landings. At this point, we have no choice; they must be taken out. DJ has uncovered enough evidence to prove they have earned this ten times over. Mitch and Mark will head up the stairs and wait at the top for Dom's signal."

They looked up expectantly, their eyes steady. Peters had a puzzled look on his face.

Jared went on to explain that he and Dom had reconnoitered the entire area and had selected the location that Dom would use to take the shots. The location, about a block and a half away, was one floor higher, giving Dom a clear shot at the Iceman's terrace.

"The building is for sale and I've gotten permission to send in two people to assess it; I went through several shadow corporations so they won't be able to identify us from that," said Jared. He looked around the room. "I didn't get where I am playing by the rules," he said.

He got nods of agreement.

"Dom and Peters are going in dressed as businessmen carrying briefcases. Except that Dom's will carry his rifle and Peters' will hold his scope."

Peters spoke up. "Isn't that a pretty long shot?"

Dom leaned over and looked at him, and he could see the

look on Peters' face. "From two hundred and fifty meters, I can reach out and touch him," he said. Peters looked back and believed him.

Jared continued. "You will all be in disguise and wearing makeup."

"Oh, no," said Mitch, "I don't have to look like a sixty-year-old man again, do I?"

"No," said Jared. "How would you like to be Polish?"

"Shit," said Mitch. "After all of the Polish jokes I've cracked, I won't be able to go into a bar and walk out alive."

"I'll carry you," said Mark.

The tensioned eased and they all laughed.

"What about us?" asked Dom.

"You are going to be Asian-Americans. You, Dom, are going to be the first Italian Asian-American."

"Can you imagine what my mother would say if she found out about this?" Dom joked.

"Then don't tell her."

"Yeah, right. She'll find out. She finds out everything. The CIA should put her on retainer."

"And I'm going to be the Indian chauffeur. 'Thank you very much, I am very glad to be taking you wherever you want to go," Jared said in a stilted but believable accent.

"Enough," he finally said. "Mitch and Mark grab the girl, bustle her into the stairwell, get dressed, and whisk her down the elevator and into the waiting limo. We'll pick up Dom and Peters and we're out of there."

Jared ended the meeting. "Melanie and DJ will anonymously dump the data we have on the Iceman to the FBI, and they can take it from there. First, however, I want Stanley to share the data indirectly with his friend at the Russian Embassy, who might—or might not—take appropriate action."

He chuckled, "Thinking back, though, I do owe the ambassador a favor."

Chapter 22

Plot and Counterplot

DEE WAS GROWING ACCUSTOMED TO the almost-daily conference calls with Melanie. Immediately following Mary Rose's visit proclaiming to be an art dealer prepared to search for old Italian masters, it became obvious to everyone that Dee had to be the one to set the bait. In fact, that is what precipitated her second visit to Klaus, requesting the loan of his painting. And, not only had he accepted, he had joined the planning sessions with something approaching youthful vigor.

Dee was both pleased and surprised to see him walk into the Galleria D right before noon the next day. Dressed in slim-fitting jeans, a white button-down shirt, and cream-colored Gucci blazer, he was the picture of elegance. His trim build belied his years, and his thick, white hair was carefully trimmed and styled. Dee complimented him on his appearance. "I wanted to whistle, Klaus, but I thought it might not be well received," she joked. "You're handsome enough to paint."

"I wouldn't have minded, my dear," he replied calmly, a smile on his face. "Now, we have work to do, don't we?" And he pulled out a slim leather folio and unzipped it.

"First," he started, "here is a copy of the original article that was written about the *Lady in Lace* before the war. Remember I told you about it? It's the only photograph in existence of the painting, and the article also describes the painting's dimensions, the techniques used, and much more."

Dee nodded, not quite sure yet where Klaus was going with this.

"Do you have an overnight envelope? We are going to send this copy off to the main office of the Boston Public Library right now. And can we put a small note with it? Not on gallery paper, of course. Let's tell them to make sure that anyone who comes in to do research about the *Lady in Lace* is shown this article—or better yet, given a copy. What do you think? Will that help your cause?"

Dee brightened immediately. "Of course. What a great idea, Klaus!"

The article was quickly dispatched, and Klaus continued. "Now, let's go over our story together. You do need to call that horrid woman back soon, don't you?" Dee nodded. "Of course, you do. Now, let's go over exactly how you are going to present this idea to—what's her name, again—Maria Rosa? You will need to demonstrate a certain reticence about passing this assignment to her. Be sure to advise her that this is no easy task, but if she finds this wondrous work of art, the rewards will be..."

Klaus stopped and smiled at Dee, who was busily taking notes.

"Tell her that it would make her wealthy beyond her wildest dreams. That should reel her in like a big fish, don't you think?" Klaus sat back in his chair, laughing heartily, seeming pleased with his own joke.

Dee came up for air, and for the first time in three days, she laughed too.

"Now, my dear," Klaus continued when he'd composed himself. "We need to give special attention to how we are going to orchestrate the night of the big reveal."

"I never even gave that a thought," said Dee.

"Oh, but my dear, that will be the supreme moment of this little affair, don't you think? We must make this a night to remember! Now, let's go out to lunch and plan our little gala."

Two hundred miles away in Boston, Mary Rose was also doing some planning—but, unlike Dee, she was alone.

It was August already, and in a little more than a week she would be on her way to Sicily. Although she was rushing around nonstop, she felt as though she wasn't getting anywhere. All day, every day, one thought was uppermost in her mind. Two days went by, then three, since her trip to New York. *When will Dee call? She just has to call. When will that call come?* Time was running short. If Dee didn't call her soon, she would lose the chance to use this trip as her excuse for finding the painting. She could be delayed by several months.

And, then, on the fourth day, the call finally came. Mary Rose was put on hold as Helen transferred the call to her; but, when it came, it was worth the wait. The assignment was huge! She knew because that's what Dee had told her. "Find this work of art and you will be rich beyond your wildest dreams." *Mind-blowingly rich!*

Mary Rose couldn't wait to see what she could find out about this very special painting, which is exactly what she did as soon as she got away from her business associates. By now, she was quite familiar with the workings of the research department at the public library, so she put in her request and took a seat at one of the tables. In a short time, a folder was placed neatly in front of her. It contained a single article about the artist and the painting. She leafed through it quickly and made her way back to the desk to speak to the woman who'd handled her request.

"You're bringing me more information, right?" Mary Rose asked, somewhat imperiously.

"No; that is all we have on this topic. Would you like me to make you a copy? That will be twenty cents for each black and white page, plus one dollar for each color page."

"If that's all you have, I guess I will take a copy," she said, almost nastily, now eager to retrieve the article and be free of this oppressively quiet sanctuary.

Ten minutes later, she hurried down the library steps and blended in with the crowd of office workers and tourists. An hour later, she stepped out of a cab at Quincy Market. Mary Rose's timing was perfect. The woman she knew only as "Wang" was packing up her canvasses and brushes, and was about to load them into a nearby van of indeterminate age and color.

Mary Rose interrupted her as she trudged toward her vehicle. "I want to talk to you, miss," she said. The painter pointedly ignored her and continued to load her things into the van. Mary Rose tried again. "You are the artist I see here every day, right? I need to talk to you."

Wang slammed the door of the van shut and glared at Mary Rose. "Come tomorrow. I'm here every day at ten in the morning, and I'm here until five, okay?"

"No," said Mary Rose, starting to become annoyed. "We are going to talk right now." Seeing that things still weren't going her way, she tried a different tack and offered to take Wang to a nearby snack bar for something to eat. "This is important." The painter relented, looking sullen, but followed her. She found a corner table and they sat down. As soon as she had Wang seated, she tried a more conciliatory tone. She found out that Wang's given name was Vivian, that her parents were Chinese, but she had grown up in New York City.

"Well, Vivian," she continued, "how would you like to make a lot of money? A whole lot of money in a very short time?"

Vivian nodded for her to continue and sipped her water.

"You cannot do this work here in the market, and you cannot tell anyone about it—ever. You will create a masterpiece from an old photograph."

"How much money?" asked Vivian.

"How soon can you get it done?" came the reply. "The faster

you paint it, the more I will pay you. For starters, you will be able to push that old van of yours into the bay and buy yourself a new one."

Vivian Wang huffed, and then she stood up. "This conversation is over. You have no idea what you are talking about."

Mary Rose stood up too, yelling "What?" over the now-noisy diners and followed Wang out of the restaurant. "Then let's find someplace quieter where we can talk."

Half an hour later and a block away, they were again seated in a corner booth where they were sure they could not be overheard, this time with drinks in their hands.

"Go on," insisted Mary Rose. "I need this painting—and I need it quickly."

"That is obvious," said Vivian, glaring at her again. "And the more you need it, the higher my price goes."

This time, she let the seconds tick by, creating the drama she needed to drag Mary Rose into her web.

"A quarter of a million dollars."

"No!"

"Yes!" she almost whispered it. "This is not some pretty painting you want for your living room. You are going to sell it to the highest bidder at, what, two million, three million dollars? I want my cut, too."

Mary Rose was dumbfounded into silence.

"This is not the tiny Chinese woman in the mall putting finishing touches on Sunflowers for customer in blue dress. This is art forgery, grand larceny. I can go to jail for that." She waited as this sunk in, and then added, "And you, too, fancy lady. You go to jail, too, for a very long time."

"Not if we don't get caught," Mary Rose replied, beginning to regain her composure.

"Now, about my money," came Wang's reply. "Do we have a deal?"

"I need to think," said Mary Rose, stalling for time. She needed to think, she needed to figure out where and how to put together a quarter of a million-dollar payment—no, payoff. "Tomorrow, here at the same time—six sharp, okay?"

"Six sharp," came the reply.

In the next booth, Carly sat still as a statue, calmly sipping her water, shocked at what she had just overheard. She waited until her surveillance subjects had cleared the area, and then she stepped outside and reached for the cell phone in her pocket. Her hunch had paid off.

Melanie took the call at home, at about 7 p.m. She praised Carly for her perseverance on her first real surveillance job. This was an amazing piece of reconnaissance since it not only proved that her team was on the right track, but it also gave them the direction they needed to plan their counterattack.

She couldn't wait to tell Dee and Jared.

Chapter 23

Sicilian Summer

MARY ROSE WAS INDISTINGUISHABLE FROM the other first-class passengers boarding the Alitalia flight to Rome. She had dressed comfortably but neatly in designer jeans, pairing them with a silk shirt, navy blazer, and tan loafers. Her solid gold necklace, matching handbag, and carry-on were elegant, but also the norm for this international set. She took her seat and pulled out a small notebook containing her recent notes, plus names and addresses of her contacts in the US and in Italy. She scanned it, returned it to her purse, leaned back, and closed her eyes, thinking back on the past ten days.

In the end, she had closed the deal with Vivian Wang, but what a tough little negotiator the woman had turned out to be. *She-devil!* Mary Rose thought it would be easy. *Offer her fifty grand. If she turns it down, make it a hundred. Easy, right?* Mary Rose now understood that she had exposed her own soft underbelly by letting Wang know how badly she needed this deal—his painting—so Wang had her over a fucking barrel. She was angry at herself for that. But now it was too late.

She'd even called Dee and told her she had an excellent lead on the painting and was going to Sicily to check it out. She'd lied, of course, telling Dee that her "sources" had told her how the artist had given several paintings to his aunt, who had brought them to Sicily before the war. And that she was on her way to go through the attic of the two-hundred-year-old family farmhouse before it went on the market. She was almost positive, she told

Dee, that she would hit "pay dirt." Dee had praised her efforts, telling her that she appreciated her dedication and wished her success in her search.

Mary Rose woke briefly as the jetliner reached first place in the lineup at Logan International and lifted into the night sky. Only one thing was causing her sleepless nights. In the end, she could not take the money out of the company coffers, so she was forced to use one of her father's financial "colleagues" to get the money she had transferred into Wang's account the week before. In one month, she would owe that dreadful man three hundred thousand dollars. Since Dee herself had assured her that "money was no object" where this particular painting was concerned, she had gone ahead and closed the deal. If she thought about how much she owed the loan shark—and what would happen if she couldn't pay him back—she would totally derail. So she concentrated instead on getting the details right. "The devil's in the details," she repeated over and over to herself, like a mantra.

She knew that old Joseph, her Papa, had no idea she was in this deal up to her neck. When she bid him good-bye, he had wished her a good trip and tucked the various gift-wrapped family trinkets and her mother's prayer book into her carry-on. Then he had kissed her on both cheeks and told her "Andare con Dio."

When the cabin steward came around she ordered a Rusty Nail. Before she'd finished her drink, she was sound asleep, her head leaning awkwardly against the cabin window. When she woke up, they were on their final descent into Rome.

Three hours later she landed at the Aeroporto de Palermo, and in a short time, she found herself speeding along in a taxi on the coast highway into town, headed to the Hotel Paradiso on the Piazza Rivoluzione. She had no illusions about the accommodations in Sicily, having been forewarned about the dirt, the noise, and possibly bed bugs in even the most expensive hotels. She knew, however, that staying with her relatives would be far worse. For certain their apartments were hot and cramped, and some elderly relative would have to be displaced from their room to make a place for her. Besides, she would not have the privacy she needed to come and go as she pleased and to make phone calls—both of which were essential to the success of her visit.

By this time, it was late Saturday afternoon, and Mary Rose was suffering greatly from jet lag, so she showered and stretched out on the bed to rest. When she woke up it was the middle of the night; for a few minutes she listened to building noises and street sounds, and then fell back asleep, a vague unease tugging at the back of her brain.

Then it was Sunday morning, and she could see from her hotel window that many of the city folk were walking to mass. Mary Rose called her Aunt Adele, certain that everyone would soon be home from church and getting ready for Sunday lunch; and, of course, she was their honored guest.

The small dining room was warm and crowded with family; the smells coming from the kitchen were unimaginably good. Mary Rose smiled for the first time since her arrival in Italy. Her grasp of the language was childish, but no one seemed to mind. Everyone wanted to welcome her to Palermo and to hug her— sometimes over and over again. She was the first person from America to visit them in twenty years, and Adele had brought out the best china for the occasion.

For a woman who seldom showed any emotion, Mary Rose found herself hugging everyone back, smiling, and replying to her greeters with the kindest words she knew. She counted twelve guests in all, from several toddlers to an elderly man who never left his chair in the corner. She thought to herself, he's probably the aging uncle who lives in the spare bedroom. He looked ancient but was probably about ninety.

One of the younger men passed around glasses of red wine and then proposed a toast. "To our American cousin, welcome. Our house is your house. Now, let's enjoy this wonderful lunch." They raised their glasses and clinked, and sat down to a feast that included plate after plate of meats and pasta, all smothered in sauce.

As the meal progressed, and more wine was consumed, Mary Rose began to understand who was who in this noisy family. Adele, her father's only surviving sister, had been a widow for many years. She was a small woman, but clearly the commanding presence in the household. There were three sons: the oldest, Giancarlo, and the twins, Adriano and Aldo. Giancarlo, who everyone called Carlo, was the only married one, and the toddlers were his. His wife was shy, quietly attending to the needs of the children. Sure enough, the old man was Adele's late husband's father. Several cousins rounded out the group, apparently regulars at the Sunday table, having no other place to go. She thought they probably lived in rented rooms while they went to school in town or worked at low-paying jobs.

By the time coffee was served, the guests had started to trickle out, leaving only the immediate family, all of whom appeared to be pleasantly full and happy. Mary Rose brought out the gifts, and with very little ceremony, placed them into her aunt's hands. The offering apparently came as no surprise, because Adele hastily thanked her for delivering the items from her brother.

Mary Rose then watched with interest as her aunt pointedly selected the wrapped prayer book and presented it to her eldest son, who stood, bowed in his mother's direction, and sat down again. Unsure as to what she had just observed, she made a mental note to report this to her father when she returned home. She was almost sure he had intended the prayer book to go to Adele and not be passed on to one of her children.

Soon after, Carlo offered to drive her back to the hotel, so she said her good-byes and accepted a ride from him; he drove his tiny car skillfully through the narrow Palermo streets for the short distance. On the way, she tried to make conversation, asking him what he did for a living. "Shipping and finance," came his terse reply.

It had been a long and interesting day, she thought, but also perplexing. *What was that little ceremony between Aunt Adele and Giancarlo? Or did it not mean anything at all?* She shrugged her shoulders and prepared for bed. As she removed her makeup, the thought crossed her mind that this was probably the most normal day she'd had in a long time.

Little did she know how wrong she was.

Once the house was quiet and the pots were soaking, Adele removed her apron and reached for the phone. Quickly she dialed the long phone number, entering the codes for the US and then for Boston.

"Talk," came the voice at the other end of the line.

"Thank you, my brother," said Adele. "I have prepared Carlo for this day since he was a boy."

"I know," said Joseph with a heartfelt sigh. "You have done a good job. Be proud of what you have accomplished with the boy. I never thought this day would come so soon, but, as you know, it has."

Joseph clicked his phone shut, closed his eyes and let his head roll back against the soft leather of his chair. It had to be done; he knew that.

He thought back to the first few days after Jonathan's death. He felt as though he'd nearly died himself, so great was the pain at his loss. Yes, his son was a wastrel, but family was family and love was love. For months, he'd buried himself at home, shut himself away in a dark room, speaking to almost no one, and opening the door only to accept the occasional visitor, or to allow his housekeeper to bring him something to eat. He wanted nothing to do with the day-to-day operation of his business and had let Mary Rose run it for him.

There would be flashbacks to that awful night every time he tried to sleep. He would see the tableau of the people in the room, standing there, guns pointed—and shots being fired. Shots that had killed his only son.

Every once in a while, the fog would lift and he would remember that something was wrong, something was very wrong. It was like the puzzles his children used to play with so many years ago. Sometimes there would be a piece missing or someone would try to put a piece where it didn't belong, and they would try to force it, twisting it and turning it to make it fit. That's what was happening in his head: a missing piece or worse. And then he would forget about it for a while until it came back to him in his dreams, over and over again.

After several months, Joseph decided to pay a visit to his office. His secretary of many years, Ginny, treated him like visiting royalty. He accepted her ministrations with grace, once and for all understanding how many people had suffered along with him. Then, uncharacteristically, she asked if she could come into his private sanctum to talk to him—alone. She wanted to confess something, and she needed Joseph's full attention. What she told him was so shocking that at first he refused to believe her. He had shouted, "No! This cannot be." And then he realized it was the only answer.

There was only one person who had deliberately sought to find out where he would be that night. And only one person who could have informed her brother of that fact. Suddenly the pieces of the puzzle fell together. And at that moment, Joseph's heart broke. Now he had lost both of his children.

Having completed her father's business, Mary Rose moved on to her personal project, satisfied that she had selected her Sicilian business partner very carefully. Now she was finally going to meet her in person. The lady in question, who was named Angela Conti, owned an art gallery, but the bulk of her work was performed in an office near the port, where she dealt with high-paying projects that needed to be shielded from the prying eyes of the public. Her specialty was documentation and transport, and most of it was of the illegal kind. Mary Rose thought the two of them would get along famously.

Angela greeted her warmly, offered her a comfortable chair, and brought out tiny cups of sweet Italian coffee. She opened Mary Rose's folder and began to spread out her notes and the paperwork. Everything was ready, which pleased Mary Rose, who considered herself to be a good judge of character, especially of "shady characters," she thought to herself, smugly.

Vivian, the Boston street artist turned forger, had already been in contact with Angela, and the *Lady* would arrive from Boston on Thursday, carefully encased in a bulky wooden box to avoid damaging the work of art; the shipping documents stated simply, "canvasses and art supplies."

Angela had the painting's shipping and export documents ready and invited Mary Rose to look over the paperwork. One of the benefits of having a gallery, Angela had explained, was that she had access to paintings she could put in front of the one that was really being shipped. That way, if any customs officer decided to open the crate and look for himself, he would see a simple painting made by a local artist, not a well-known famous painting. The ruse had worked well in the past, and there was no reason to believe it would be otherwise this time.

Mary Rose followed Angela into the workroom, where they examined the frame and the crate, so she could see how it all went together. Then, with somewhat of a flourish, Angela produced her masterpiece: the forged provenance for *Lady in Lace*. This elegant-looking document would be the "proof" that the masterpiece was what it purported to be: a painting worth several million dollars. It verified the artist as correct, and traced the history of the canvas, guaranteeing that it had been in Italy for the past eighty years. Mary Rose whistled her approval.

"Well done, my new friend," she said. "I'd like to take you to lunch to celebrate our partnership. Do you have a favorite restaurant?"

"Yes, I do," replied Angela. "I'd like that very much. All this hard work has given me an appetite."

The rest of the week passed by pleasantly enough for Mary Rose, who hadn't felt so relaxed and carefree since her college days. She slept late, sipped tiny cups of sweet coffee at outdoor cafes with rickety tables and flower boxes full of geraniums, and poked around in the shops, picking up trinkets to bring home to America. She had almost forgotten about the huge hole she'd dug for herself—and when the thought reared its ugly head, she did her best to ignore it.

She made return visits to her aunt's home, one time for lunch, and another for coffee. However, she could not get past what she felt was a barrier. It was as if Adele had deliberately created an emotional wall between them. Oh, well, she thought. *There is nothing I can do about that.*

She and Angela had also met again. The first time they'd met at her office, on Friday, after the painting had arrived from Boston. They opened it together, sharing their eagerness and hope that the copy of *Lady in Lace* would meet their expectations. And it did!

"Your artist does excellent work, Mary Rose! This painting—this fake—is amazing. It is beautifully done."

"Thank you," she replied, beaming. "I think I have found a very talented artist."

"This is one of those games we could play again if the opportunity arises, don't you think?" asked Angela.

"Oh, yes," said Mary Rose. "In fact, I am counting on it."

"Well, then, you can count me in." came the reply.

"I think we have ourselves a winner," said Mary Rose. "I value your opinion, and I think—no, I know—this will fly. We have produced a fake masterpiece, complete with all the trimmings. And there is no doubt in my mind that this is foolproof."

The co-conspirators met one more time—for dinner. That night they laughed and drank way too much wine, and she thought that if circumstances were different, their friendship could have blossomed into so much more. By the end of the week, Mary Rose had forgotten all about looking for that elusive Italian lover and was basking in the warm camaraderie of her newfound friend.

And, then, before she knew it, her Sicilian vacation was over, and she was buckling her seat belt for the first leg of her trip back to Boston. *Arrivederci. I can't wait to come back to Sicily.*

Chapter 24

Can They Rescue Lucy?

P ETERS WAS WITH DOM ON the roof of the building selected for the shoot. It was a long way from the Iceman's penthouse. Peters still couldn't believe he had been asked to come along.

"Do you want to be in on it when we get her back?" Dom had asked him.

Peters hadn't hesitated, "Yes, LT, I damn well do."

"All right, I'm the shooter; you're the spotter. Do you have a problem with that?"

"No, sir! I've looked down the barrel of a gun before and pulled the trigger."

"Good. Your job is to identify the targets for me in the right order for elimination."

"Yes, sir!" Peters was in this all the way and knew that Dom wanted him to see the steel in Protek. Peters wondered how Dom could hit a barn door from this far away but decided he'd keep that thought to himself.

Dom had the twelfth-floor penthouse roof in his sights. He noted the low glass railing around the terrace, the potted plants dotting the area, and the small oval swimming pool. Nothing he saw would prove to be any problem in getting off his shots. He had a clear field of fire straight to the two lounge chairs where he hoped his subjects would lie down to sunbathe.

A few minutes after they'd settled in, the penthouse's sliding glass doors opened and a tall, thin, blond man came out followed by a young girl—and they were both naked. They were accompanied by two men who stood guard, one on each side of the door.

"Is that her?" asked Dom.

"Yes, LT."

"Are you sure?"

"Yes! I'll never forget the moment when they grabbed her; those two are the ones who did it. I've been living with that, thinking I should have been able to stop it, but I wasn't there in time."

"Well, now you are, First Sergeant. Give me a target."

Peters took a deep breath and looked through his scope. "The one on the left is the man who grabbed her; the one on the right is the guy who ran the op, and he has his hand on his gun. Take him first."

Dom adjusted his sights—it was a little windy from left to right today. Then he spoke into his mic/earpiece. "Subjects on the roof. SITREP."

Mitch came back immediately with the situation report. "We're in the subject's building and in place. First two subjects down and unconscious. The elevator codes DJ got for us worked. We're on the tenth floor, where the main elevator ends. From here we have to hoof it two flights to the pool deck."

Mitch and Mark had already stripped down to their bathing suits and stood waiting with towels over their arms, guns hidden in the folds. "There are two more guards here, one on each landing. We can take them out next."

"Tell me when you're ready," said Dom into his mic.

Mitch quietly climbed the stairs to the eleventh-floor landing. The man there looked at him and did a double take. "Who the hell are you?"

"The boss said we could use the pool," said Mitch as he came up the stairs with Mark behind him. The man on the top floor looked over the railing to see what was going on.

"Like hell!" were the last words each of them ever said or heard as Mitch and Mark shot them both with silenced polycarbonate Glocks.

"Clear," said Mitch quietly into his mic.

On the roof, the man on the right suddenly started to slump. His partner wasn't all that quick and didn't notice at first. But when he looked he saw the tiny red dot, a little to the left and above his right eye, he got the message. He reached for his gun.

"Damn wind," said Dom quietly. He didn't change the sights, but he did correct his aim ever so slightly. The second man went down with the red dot dead centered between his eyes.

The Iceman still hadn't noticed anything. He was gently fondling Lucy's breast and still trying to decide if he would sell her or keep her. After all, he didn't need the money.

Dom's third shot hit him in the knee. As the pain hit him, he twisted around to see where his bodyguards were, but they were already dead—and that's when he realized he had only moments to live. He looked wildly around to see where the shots came from.

He reached down into his bag and pulled out a pistol.

"Jesu Cristi, LT," said Peters in awe.

"Survival mirror!"

Peters took the mirror from his breast pocket. It was polished steel with a hole in it so it could be aimed at rescue airplanes.

Dom racked another round into the rifle. "Show him where we are so he knows what's about to happen. I want him to think about this for a little while before I give this bastard a one-way ticket to hell."

Peters aligned the mirror with the sun and a bright spot of light shone right in the Iceman's eyes.

The Iceman couldn't believe how far away the shots were coming from. He started to swing his gun toward Lucy but watched in horror as his right wrist exploded.

Although the Iceman would never know it, Dom had anticipated his move and this bullet had already been on its way.

The Iceman dropped his head and waited for the final shot that never came. There was no need. The artery in his wrist had been opened and he was bleeding out. He tried to stop it but didn't have the strength. Slowly he lost consciousness.

His last thought was, "Кто мог бы сделать это для меня?"

Dom started to break down his rifle, carefully fitting the pieces into what looked like an executive briefcase.

"Collect the brass and we're out of here. Four shots," he said to Peters. Then he said into his mic, "Exfiltrate."

"Copy that," came back.

Mark and Mitch raced out onto the pool deck and Mark picked Lucy up in his arms. He carried her back into the stairwell, stopped, put her down gently, and wrapped a robe around her. They dressed quickly. Mitch had brought a syringe to keep Lucy sedated, but she already was, so he didn't need to use it. He slung her over his shoulder and headed downstairs, with Mark guarding his six. "Jesus!" Mark said, "Dom shot his hand off. From way over there!"

A long, black limo was waiting at the building's entrance, a disguised Jared at the wheel. They all piled in. Lucy was safe and on the first leg of her trip home, first to rehab, and then to be reunited with her family in Boston.

Peters exited the building with Dom, talking like a couple of businessmen; they watched the limo come around the corner. "Clean takedown," said Dom.

"Not quite," said Peters. "It's my turn to handle this," he said, glancing down the street. "I wasn't there in time to prevent Lucy from being grabbed, but maybe I can make some small difference here."

What Peters saw—from almost a block away—was a purse snatching about to happen. A little old lady walked toward them carrying a small bag of groceries while a scruffy young man checked to see if the coast was clear. He ran up behind the unsuspecting woman and grabbed her purse. He headed down the street, giving the businessmen the finger as he ran.

Dom stepped aside with a surprised look on his face, but Peters clotheslined the thief with a hit that would have had all the yellow flags in history out on the field if this had been an NFL game. Peters grabbed him and lifted him up, shoving him up against a brick wall until he was roughed up enough to understand that purse snatching was a bad career move. The two men searched his pockets and removed all the contents. Finally, they allowed him to drop to the sidewalk. Dom picked up the purse and walked back to the little old lady.

From the limo, Jared saw it all go down; still in his Indian accent, he said, "Oh my goodness, by all the gods and small children, look at what our friends have gotten themselves into. I am afraid I shall have to drive around the block again until they resolve the issue."

That brought a laugh from Mitch and Mark and even a tiny

smile from Lucy; she knew something funny had been said even though she had no idea what they were talking about.

Dom and Peters offered to walk the lady home. "I'd be so happy if you did," she said. "This neighborhood just isn't safe anymore."

They escorted her to her door and she turned and reached into her purse, "I'd like to give you something for your trouble," she said, "a little token of my appreciation. I'm not poor, so don't think for a moment that I'll go hungry." There was a twinkle in her eyes.

Dom and Peters looked at each other. Dom put his hand on her arm, but Peters spoke first. "It was our pleasure, ma'am."

"Well, thank you, young men, I do appreciate what you've done for me. It was so wonderful to be protected by such nice, handsome young men."

Dom and Peters exchanged looks again and smiled. Dom wondered if she would have said that had she known what they'd done in the last half hour. They waved good-bye as she headed up the steps to her brownstone. She turned one last time to see them, but what she saw was the two of them getting into a long, black limo.

"Funny, they didn't sound Japanese. I guess they won't go hungry tonight either," she said to herself.

Jared was still using his Indian accent. "Very well, young gentlemen, the job was going perfectly and then you to had rescue a lady in distress. That was not in the original plan we discussed. I am correct, I think?"

He raised his hand and changed back to his normal tone before anyone could say anything. "I would have done the same thing if you hadn't been there. Mitch and Mark were about to leap out to stop this guy too. It was the right thing to do and

I don't believe the takedown was compromised. The nice little old lady won't be able to recognize any of us, thanks to our disguises, and the real perps are dead. End of problem."

They all nodded. No matter how many times they had done it or how deserving it was, killing always left a mark on each of them.

Lucy broke their reverie. "When can I have some more fun shots? I'm starting to feel itchy."

Jared stomped down on the accelerator. "No more fun shots for you, Lucy. You're going *home*."

Joseph's cellphone buzzed; when he saw who it was, he answered respectfully. "You have news about Lucia?"

He listened as Jared gave him the details and told him when she could be expected to return home. She had been subjected to barbiturates to keep her sedated and it would take a few days to wash them out of her system. She was in a secure, guarded facility to guarantee that she would not be attacked again. While this was happening, she would also receive counseling to alleviate any emotional trauma she might have suffered, although, given the drugs she'd been on, she would probably only remember it all as a bad dream. "And remember what we talked about at the beginning? The statement has been made, and the 'person of interest' will never trouble us again."

"I thank you," said Joseph. "I will never forget your kindness. Once again, I find myself indebted to you. I expect you will also be hearing from Lucia's parents and grandparents. They will want to thank you in person. Good night, Jared."

"Good night, Joseph. Sleep well."

Chapter 25

The Aftermath

J ARED'S INTERCOM BUZZED, WHICH NEVER happened unless it was important. "Yes?" he answered.

"Stanley called," said Mickey, the receptionist. "The Russian ambassador would like a few words with you in private. He said 20:30 hours and named a local Russian restaurant. Shall I accept?"

"No need to," said Jared. "He already knows I'll be there."

"I've alerted Mitch and Mark. It's good to see them back together. How should they look?"

"I'll leave that to Mitch, but send another team in for training. The ambassador will love it, and the junior varsity will have to figure out who are friends and who are the enemies."

He heard her laugh over the intercom. She loved to live vicariously through these crazy people.

"And drop Dom into the group just for fun; let's see if he can remain hidden or if they spot him."

"So this is another field exercise?"

"No, Pyotr Stephonovich will have his best people there as well, and one of us will pay the bill. But he is serious if he called me, even discreetly."

Jared walked into the dimly lit bar and restaurant with a smile on his face. There were few patrons at this time of night in this part of town. It took him a moment to recognize Mitch and Mark, disguised as the two old men playing chess at a corner table. The bartenders gave themselves away by looking too fixedly at him: they must belong to Pyotr. He wondered where the rest were. Ah, yes, the waiters. They pranced around each other like dancers in the Nutcracker Ballet.

"Zdravstvuyte, Jared Georgovich," said his host.

"And to you, Pyotr Stephonovich," Jared replied. "And how are your wife and daughter?"

"Stephania is in the Mechinada Academica. How you say, 'The MIT of Russia.' She is doing very well."

"If there is anything I can ever do to advance her career, I would be happy to assist."

The two men looked at each other. Pyotr spoke first.

"I would not like to play chess with either of those two men."

"No, you would not. They are the best there are."

"The ones known as Mitchell and Mark?"

"Yes."

"They are legendary. I have warned my people about them and they still didn't see them."

"The bartenders and the waiters will learn in time if, as we say in the US of A, they 'make the cut.'"

Pyotr laughed. "We all have to learn, don't we?"

"Indeed," said Jared.

The two men looked at each other for another long moment. The vodka was served silently: chilled Stavka.

"Tell me about it," said Pyotr, draining his glass.

Jared tossed his down and then complimented his host on the vodka. "Stavka," he said, "I've only tasted it one time, but it can never be forgotten."

Then he explained in detail what had happened. Right down to the purse snatching. Pyotr laughed aloud. "I couldn't stop it," said Jared. "If my people hadn't taken it down, I would have done so personally."

"As would I, my friend, as would I."

Jared knew that however much Pyotr looked like Santa Claus, he was fit and someone to fear. If he had been there when the purse snatching happened, the perp would have been lucky to leave with his head still attached to his shoulders.

The dinner appeared. "A delicacy for you, a whole suckling piglet."

Jared laughed, "I have been told to warn suckling pigs about eating whole apples; they do tend to be hazardous to their health."

Pyotr roared again. The sous chef looked pointedly at him and Jared did not miss it. His assistant kept his head down and was virtually unnoticeable, but Pyotr saw the look. "Ah," he said.

"The man with the gun. He was the shooter," said Jared.

"He was doing very well until I saw his eyes. That always gives them away."

The meal was served and finally Jared asked, "Why the meeting, Pyotr Stephonovich?"

"First, to thank you for calling me about the shooting before you called your FBI."

"I thought it would not only be diplomatic, that you might find some, shall we say, threads that might lead you to the people who do this."

"Indeed, we searched the apartment and found a laptop that was apparently unaccounted for in our inventory. However, it is very well encrypted. I have a favor to ask of you." He waited for Jared to digest this. "It was a heinous crime, one which neither of us would ever want to happen to our children."

"Amen."

"I need Boris and Natasha back—I want them out of your federal prison," he said. "Have those two not done enough time already for their role in, how did you call it, the penny scam?"

Jared thought for a long moment. "Not going to happen," he

finally said. "No way the feds will let those two out on the street for the next decade."

"Pity, then I will have to rely on, as you say, the second team."

"Do you mean невидимый?" said Jared fluently.

"Da, 'invisible.' How do you know that?"

"One of my cryptographers is a friend of his. They correspond often. Would it be to our mutual benefit if we could allow them to pursue this?"

"As long as it doesn't surface in diplomatic circles."

Jared gave him a droll look. "Pyotr Stephonovich, please."

"I am confident that between the two of us we can find and exterminate these awful creatures who prey on young girls."

"Yes, we can," Pyotr agreed, "but we will never, ever be able to put a complete stop to it. However, what you have done in the last two days will make those who do it think twice. The word is out about what happens when you try to 'pet the cobra.'"

"I have no idea what you're talking about," said Jared.

"Then let us drink to a wonderful repast," said Pyotr, and they downed their second round of vodka.

The detective and his partner Jeff entered the Iceman's apartment building. They were met by a security guard who looked at their badges and appeared reluctant to admit them.

"The elevators are out of order," said the guard. "You'll have to walk up."

Detective Michael McAllister gave him a hard look. Mac, as he was known, was a devotee of Peter Falk's Columbo, right down to the rumpled shirts and pants, loose ties, and even the gray trench coat. The only thing missing was the cigar, which was no longer allowed—the Captain had prohibited smoking or even carrying them while on duty.

Looking at him, everyone expected him to stop at the last moment, raise a finger and say, 'Oh, just one more question...'

When he'd been assigned to Mac, Jeff thought he'd been thrown under the bus. Now, six months later, he realized this was the top assignment. There were some very envious recruits who told him they had wanted to work with Mac. But Mac had asked for *him*. He was only beginning to understand what this meant. Mac was tough and demanding, but he was also fair, and Jeff was learning. Faster than he ever thought he could learn.

Mac walked over to the elevators and punched in the code. The doors opened.

"How did you do that?" asked Jeff.

"A little bird told me," came the answer. Then he punched in the code and the elevator took them to the tenth floor. From there they took the stairs to the penthouse floor and began to look around. Mac spent thirty minutes examining everything. The only thing missing was his Sherlock Holmes magnifying glass.

"What do you think about this?" Mac asked.

"It's been detailed."

"Right," said Mac. "Sterilized."

They went out on the pool deck. Mac looked around for a while. "Look here," he finally said, as he pointed to a small ding in the wall. "The chair had to have been here at that time of day. There are some stains on the deck that weren't removed completely. Line them up with the ding on the wall and let's see if that gives us anything."

His apprentice did exactly that. "Way over there?"

"Yep, that must have been one *hell* of a shot."

"Damn!"

"Let's walk down to that building to see what we can find, before they shut us down."

"What do you mean?"

"It's already happened, kid; we're on borrowed time, but maybe we can find out a few things, just for fun."

They walked across the street and down the block. "Up there?"

"Yep."

"Wow!"

"Wonder if there's anything of interest here."

At that very moment, a little old lady appeared, walking down the street with her small bag of groceries. She looked apprehensive when she saw them, but when they showed her their badges, she seemed reassured.

"Last evening," asked Mac, "did you see anything unusual?"

"Oh, yes," she said, "It was so exciting! Now, I go to the store every afternoon, to get out of the house and get my exercise, you know? I walked home with my groceries, just like today, and this bad man grabbed my purse. An old lady's purse. What was he thinking? No respect for people in my generation. Anyway, he ran down the street with my purse, but these two men stopped him. Oh, did they ever. It was something out of Kung Fu. Remember that TV series? I loved Grasshopper. Well, those two nice men gave me back my purse and even walked me home."

"Did you see their faces?"

"Oh, yes, they were Asian—maybe Chinese, or Japanese."

"Could you recognize them?"

"Perhaps, but would I? The men who saved my purse? I don't think so."

Mac looked at her and nodded. "Where do you live?"

"Right around the corner, young man. They made sure I got home safely, and I thanked them profusely. I do remember they got into a black limousine..."

"Did you get the license plate number?" asked Jeff.

Mac looked at Jeff and shook his head; would this kid ever learn?

"Oh, but a little while later I looked out my front window, and two more limos showed up, and all kinds of people got out and went into that building."

"Did you get the license plate numbers?" asked Jeff again.

"No, but I think they had diplomatic plates," she said emphatically.

Mac thanked her and led his partner away.

"End of investigation," he said. "Case closed."

"Why?" asked Jeff.

"Don't even ask."

Chapter 26

The Cryptographers

G LORIA HAD JUST SETTLED DOWN next to DJ at their matching computers. It was their first night in the new flat, as she called it, and she eagerly anticipated their all night lovemaking. It was time for DJ to surrender his virginity. She tingled at the thought.

The doorbell rang. "Shoot," she said knowing that the 'Best laid plans o' mice an' men gang aft agley.' *Thank you, Robert Burns. Damn you!* She knew right then that tonight was not going to be the night.

She opened the front door to find Peters standing there, another man at his side. "Sorry to disturb you, ma'am, but this guy tells me he has an important message from невидимый." She could see that Peters had been boning up on his Russian. Gloria looked at DJ, surprised to see that he, too, recognized the reference to the Russian cryptographer.

"How can you possibly know who he is?" DJ blurted out.

"He's a phantom on the social networks that no one has ever been able to track down," she said simply.

"Well, he'd better stay that way, if he doesn't want to die a painful death," said DJ. "But, obviously, this guy knows who he is."

"I'm Steven Heber; I work in cryptology," said the newcomer, extending his hand.

Gloria had heard of this division at Protek, but no one knew where it was or who worked there. Not strange for a security company, but somebody must have thought that any knowledge of its existence would be dangerous to the employees in such a group.

"Why are you here?" Gloria asked.

"I need DJ's Cray!" Steven blurted out. "My friend in Russia has access to a laptop that has coded information about the men who have had young American girls abducted and then purchased them as sex slaves. We have gone as far as we can, but we have now encountered a firewall and an encrypted program that we cannot break. Jared told me to contact you. And please, my friend in Russia will be in grave danger if anything leaks out."

"As will you," said Gloria, taking control of the situation. "Probably, so will DJ and I. Let's get to work." She turned to her computer and watched as DJ followed her lead.

"Tell me what you've got," she demanded flatly.

Steven logged into their network. "Damn," exclaimed DJ, "this stuff is state of the art."

"Do you know what I think?" asked Gloria. "You are the best hacker on the planet, my love, but three minds are better than one."

"Ellen and Irving," he finally said.

"Yes."

"Can we trust them?" asked Steve.

"With our lives," said Gloria. "Plus, we all have top-level security clearances." She reached for the phone and gestured to DJ to clear the Cray. While she waited for Ellen to answer in Las Vegas, she said to Steven, "We also have two more computers we can access that are better than the Cray and that you don't know about, never even heard about and will certainly, I mean certainly, never mention to anyone. Have I made myself clear?"

Steven nodded, clearly respecting Gloria's authority.

Gloria spoke quietly to Peters for a moment. He nodded and

left, pulled out his cell and called for backup security on the street below. It was going to be a long night.

———————

Ellen answered her cell phone. "E and I, Whale Watching, LLC," she said sweetly. "How can we help you?"

She heard Gloria's laugh. The two had met at the last company meeting and bonded immediately.

"So I hear you've adopted a homeless pet," said Ellen.

"He needs to be housebroken," said Gloria, "but it's not beyond the realm of possibility."

"That's what I said about Irving," confided Ellen, "and it was true."

Gloria explained the situation. Ellen grabbed the remote and switched off the football game to get Irving's attention. He got the message and headed for their home office. When Ellen got there, he was already logged in and talking to DJ.

"Ellen, you're the firewall queen; we'll do our best, but it's all yours," said Gloria.

Ellen put down her cell phone and went to work. It took her twenty minutes to get through. Irving put one of their new supercomputers into the breach and cranked it up. There was a second wall, but it wasn't as good as the first. Irving put his second supercomputer into that and then DJ's Cray was in and working on the encryption program.

"Do we need a translation of the original?" asked Ellen.

"No, my friend told me it would be more accurate if I wrote a decryption program in the original language," said Steven.

"Now, you leave here and don't tell anyone that you were here, what goes on here, or what happened tonight," cautioned Gloria.

Steven gulped, "Yes, ma'am," he said as he turned and fled. *I thought what I did was scary, but these guys are out of the ballpark.*

"Now what happens?" asked Ellen. No one noticed it was 2 a.m. Eastern Standard Time.

Gloria looked around sleepily. The sun was coming up in Washington, DC.

DJ's head was in her lap—not the exact place she hoped it would be the night before, but okay for now. She thought about her friends in Las Vegas; they had the advantage of being three hours behind her, so sunrise was still not a problem for them. She smiled at that. Then she wondered what had awakened her. It was the Cray's incessant dinging. Was something wrong? She gently lifted DJ's head from her lap, stretched, and padded to the terminal.

"Oh my God!" she said. The encoding had been broken and the Cray was spitting out line after line of translated Russian. Not only were there names and addresses of the sex perverts, but there was also information about other nefarious persons and activities. Gloria didn't know where to start. She knew that the Cray was automatically saving all of this, so that wasn't a problem.

"DJ," she yelled, "come in here right away."

DJ had been in the middle of a delicious dream about sleeping with his head in Gloria's lap. She was calling him "my love," over and over again, as she had for the first time the previous evening. When she yelled, he cranked over and came alive slowly, like the starter of a cold car in February in Northern Wisconsin. When he staggered out of the bathroom he was not a pretty sight, but he was, at least, functional. He headed for his office and found Gloria staring at the computer terminal.

"Look at all of this," she exclaimed. "No wonder the Iceman

was so powerful! He had something bad on half the crooks in Russia! And the other half owed him favors!"

DJ took command. His mind cleared miraculously and he picked up the phone and speed-dialed Melanie while typing with one hand on another computer—re-routing the Cray feed to her secure terminal at the office.

At first, Melanie wasn't pleased because she had just gone back to bed after feeding Evan in the hour before dawn, and she was very short on sleep. DJ handed the phone to Gloria, who had recovered enough to explain what was going on. Melanie was instantly, well, Melanie at warp speed.

"My office in one hour," she barked. "DJ, can the Cray run by itself or do you need to be there?"

"It just stopped," he told her. "I think that's all we're gonna get from this laptop. I'll wrap it up and the code and bring it with me. I'll be happier when it's all in the vault."

"Good. Do it!" snapped Melanie. "See you in one hour; I've got calls to make. Oh, and by the way, great job."

Gloria, who was now holding on tight to DJ, could sense the smile on Melanie's face over the phone. Gloria couldn't resist; she had to kiss him.

So she did.

Jared and Pyotr raised their glasses and tossed down the excellent vodka.

"So, Jared Georgovich, we drink to a successful conclusion."

"Da, Pyotr Stephonovich, but I hope we will not sacrifice another innocent piglet for this occasion," said Jared with a smile.

"Nyet! There are enough pigs in Russia with apples in their mouths now to satisfy all of us," laughed Pyotr. "I hope they enjoy cold weather; Siberia is chilly this time of year."

"You know, Jared Georgovich, it is, as you say, a pleasure to do business with you. You told me what you could do and you did it. That is rare in my homeland. I hope we can work together again."

"One thousand an hour is my normal rate, but for you, Pyotr Stephonovich, nine-hundred ninety-nine. A special deal."

Pyotr laughed again. "Rubles or dollars?" he asked.

"We take only Euros from our Eastern Allies," said Jared.

That brought another laugh. "You capitalists never give up, do you?"

"Seriously," he continued, "I have a favor to ask of you. It concerns the cryptologist who assisted your man. I have been informed that two plots have already been discovered to assassinate him, which, fortunately, were nipped in the bud, as you Americans say. However, sooner or later, one such plot will succeed. We should not lose such a valuable asset. He would like to come to America. Is there any way you can put him in your 'Work Release Program?'"

Jared smiled, "You know, of course, that it's the Witness Protection Program, Pyotr Stephonovich, but I'll forgive you for that; and no, as a private company, I can't get him into that program, but yes, I'll be happy to help you. I do have the re-sources to make him disappear completely and be reborn as a Protek employee. He might even undergo some minor plastic surgery—then his own mother wouldn't recognize him. Does he have family that I should include?"

"A son, one and a half years old; his wife died in childbirth. A credit to our progressive medical system," he said sarcastically. "Both parents dead. I will finance this personally."

"No need, my friend; he will earn his own living, and then some. Not all of the pigs with apples in their mouths are in your homeland. And I will find someone to care for his son."

"I assume that your friend who is high up in the government will be discreet about the information."

Jared didn't even blink; his host vowed never to play poker with him.

"Who?" asked Jared.

A waiter appeared with two racks of venison with juniper berry sauce.

"I had them flown in from Siberia," said Pyotr. "It is so cold there that the deer cannot wait to get into a warm oven."

Chapter 27

Gloria's One Desire

GLORIA AND DJ HAD NOW been in the new apartment for several weeks, but due to their conflicting work schedules, they had hardly been at home together. They shared a bed, affectionately, but they still hadn't consummated their relationship. It was far from the romantic home life Gloria had so hopefully envisioned. *I should have known*, she thought one morning as she drove to work, alone again.

The apartment had come together nicely in the end and hadn't taken long either. Gloria remembered what her father used to say: "Throw enough money at a problem and you can make it go away." Well, that's what they had done with the painters, the upholsterers, the carpet people, and all of the other service providers. People came and quietly hooked up the smart TV and networked the computers.

Now, all she really wanted was to spirit DJ away from work long enough to give her his undivided attention. In the end, she decided to enlist Melanie's help. Mel called DJ into her office and told him he looked like he hadn't slept for a month and to go home and not come back for three whole days.

That's how Gloria finally got her long weekend. Now to her plan to make DJ her own.

As she discovered the next morning, DJ had no idea what to do with a day off—much less three entire days. He hadn't taken a vacation in a decade. It was a beautiful, late-summer day, so she invited him to go for a walk in the neighborhood. She took his hand and began to point out the interesting sights. They walked as far as Starbucks where DJ had his wallet out as soon as he spotted the familiar sign. A few minutes later, they were sitting outside at a wrought-iron table, sipping skim-milk lattes.

"So, my love, what would you like to do today?" she asked him.

"Well, Mel did ask me to look into something..." he began.

"Sweetie, today is a work-free zone. What Mel wants, and what I need, is for you to take it easy for a few days. You've worked so hard recently that you're still running on a huge 'high.' It's time for you to come down off that high and relax a little."

When he started to object, she hit below the belt.

"I guarantee you that Jared takes time off, and I know Mitch enjoys his weekends."

"Yeah, I guess so," came his reply, half-questioning. "But what do they *do*?"

"They start," she replied simply, "by taking time to enjoy the women in their lives."

On the way back to the flat, they stopped at an Asian market where Gloria picked up some unrecognizable ingredients. The fishmonger was next, and more items were selected, wrapped, and paid for. They arrived back home, laughing, as DJ tried to guess what was on the menu for dinner. Obviously, it was outside his normal food groups of tacos and pizza, but Gloria knew he was beginning to trust her skill in the kitchen.

She led him into the bedroom and began to remove her clothes. She tossed away her windbreaker; then she sat down on the bed and slipped off her sneakers and sweats. She invited DJ to do the same, tossing his items in the direction of the laundry basket. Now, totally naked, she walked delicately toward the shower. As she moved, she pulled her hair on top of her head, forming a loose knot. She stepped into the large glass shower stall and turned on the water jets, one by one. Gloria was a woman on a mission, and she wouldn't rest until DJ was all hers.

DJ followed her into the shower, his eyes drawn to her swaying backside. He thought she was the most beautiful woman on the planet. That was his last rational thought for many hours. From that moment on, Gloria bombarded his senses until he could no longer have told her his name, had she asked, but, of course, she didn't. He noticed that she had filled the shower with sweet-smelling products, and did not realize they were all designed to put even the most reluctant of bodies in the mood for love.

Used to taking quickie showers, DJ suddenly found himself under Gloria's ministrations. Her hands were all over his body, rubbing, massaging, rinsing, and—yes—exploring. Without knowing exactly what he was doing, DJ began to follow suit. He picked up a fragrant soap and began rubbing it on a sea sponge, watching as it foamed. He began to run the sponge gingerly up and down her body, and then around her middle. Spurred on by her encouragement, he drew the sponge first around one small breast, and then the other. He caught on, turned her around, and carefully traced the outline of her firm backside with his little magic sponge.

He drew her close and saw the look in her eyes change from one of playfulness to one of arousal. Then he looked down and felt, rather than saw, his own. It was a feeling of wonderment and power, all at the same time. This tiny woman had done to him what no one had ever done before: he was a man in love—about to take this amazing woman to bed and make her his own.

Chapter 28

Rock the Boat

THE END OF SUMMER MEANT it was time to sail *Chauffeuse* to Norfolk, Virginia from her current location in Bermuda, where she'd remained ever since the race ended. The crew had enjoyed a peaceful few weeks, taken out a few charter guests, and were now readying the boat for the trip home. Jared told Barney to tell the crew they could take off their last night in Bermuda.

He'd said, "Let them go to dinner, have a few drinks, and generally, blow off steam before the trip, and make sure no one gets in trouble." Barney had asked Jared for the night off, too, but he planned to stay on board. He was sending Scott into town with the rest of the crew, mainly to keep tabs on them. He didn't object to his crew having a good time, but he wanted to make sure no one started a fight or broke things. They were the best crew in town, so he was pretty sure there wouldn't be any trouble. It was a beautiful evening, and Barney watched as his freshly washed and more or less clean-shaven sailors left the boat, laughing and bantering.

Now there was only one other person left on board with Barney: Brianna. Barney had told Jared about that plan, too, and Jared had shared the information with Dee. Her message to Barney was, "Have yourselves a bottle of champagne—on us. Jared will tell you where the key to the private liquor locker is. You two have most certainly earned it. And, you guys have our blessing."

At the moment, Barney was sitting on the aft deck, a beer in his hand, waiting for Brianna, who had gone below to take a shower after a full day's work. She'd gone into town and purchased all the food and sundries the crew needed for the trip, and then come back to *Chauffeuse* and stored everything in the galley. On any other boat, that would have taken two crew members; for her, it was an easy one-woman job.

As Brianna stepped into the shower, her thoughts turned to the past few weeks. She couldn't remember when she'd had a better time in her life. She was almost thirty years old and had spent most of her years since high school working on boats. And, not merely working, but working hard—very hard. If there was a problem to be handled, it was always, "Don't worry; Brianna will take care of it."

That's why the past few weeks had seemed like a luxury vacation to her. Every day the crew did some light maintenance on the boat, but it was easy duty. She even had time to shop in town. As a result, her tiny wardrobe had a few pairs of new shorts, some brightly colored t-shirts, and a nightie; she'd even added a tinted lip gloss and a mascara.

And to what did she owe the impromptu shopping trip? Well, she was hopeful that the sideways glances she'd received from Barney over the past few weeks meant more than friendship.

A girl can hope, can't she?

For about the hundredth time this summer, Barney had thanked his lucky stars for his job with Jared at the boatyard, and for his life crewing *Chauffeuse*. He couldn't have asked for more if he'd been given "carte blanche" to invent his life from scratch. For years, he'd gone from boat to boat and always felt that something was missing. With Jared, this crew, and this boat, he'd finally found what he considered to be home.

This most recent Bermuda race had clinched what he'd always known about Jared: the man was his hero. And he wasn't a hero in a showy way; he was, quite simply, a man of honor, the kind of person who did the right thing—whether anyone was looking or not. He thought back to other captains he'd worked for and knew for a fact that no one even came close to Jared. And the way he went to save *Harmony* and her crew had proved his point. These days he was a proud and happy man.

There was only one thing missing in his life, and it was only in the past few weeks that he'd even taken the time to think about it: and he had Brianna to thank for that. Brianna, hard worker, strong and determined, always cheerful and full of life. He knew she'd had some tough times in the past, but she never complained, and never dwelled on the negatives. Her last skipper had treated her really badly, and she had simply walked away, giving him the finger as she jumped off his boat for the last time. Her work ethic and energy matched his own. He respected her. But, his man-brain sensed the sexual tension between them, and he hoped that tonight she would show him a different side—her womanly side.

Brianna emerged on deck, freshly showered, with her blonde, damp hair slicked back. She had on white shorts and a pink t-shirt that did as much as was humanly possible to show off her body. She was, in fact, a bit of a fireplug, never having had the much sought after hourglass figure, but she made up for that with boundless energy and enthusiasm. Like Barney, she had chosen a cold beer. She found a second deck chair, pulled it next to his, and sat down to watch the sunset with him. For a few minutes, they sat in silence while they enjoyed their drinks, the quiet, and the beauty of the ocean.

Barney spoke first. "It won't be easy to leave this place. Bermuda is really beautiful. Don't you love it here, Brianna?"

"I do," she replied. "This is the closest I've come to a vacation in many years. And now, tonight, we have the boat to ourselves, don't we? Where did everyone go?"

"I gave them all the night off. They seemed happy to go. I hope they don't end the evening by getting drunk and breaking up some bar."

"Oh, I think they'll behave, don't you? They're a good crew. The best I've ever sailed with."

"Well, Scott can keep them under control," said Barney. "Now, the charcoal is hot in the Magma grill on the stern; down in the galley, I've got a couple of steaks ready to slap on it, a salad that's already been tossed, and baked potatoes in the microwave. Just for the two of us. How does that sound to you, Brianna?"

"It sounds like heaven, Barney," she answered. "I thought you'd never ask."

Barney finished dinner with Brianna by his side; they had loaded their plates in the galley and took them back on deck. They ate their meal as the sun set and washed it all down with a bottle of red wine from Jared and Dee's special cabinet.

As they ate, they chatted about how to set the staysail and the spinnaker, and by the time they'd finished their meal—and the bottle of wine—they were talking about the important things in their lives: like what made them happy, what made them sad, how they felt about friendship and closeness and loyalty, and what they needed from a "special someone." By the time it was dark on deck, Barney had his arm around Brianna, and she reached over, tentatively, and kissed him. He returned the kiss and upped the ante. Twenty minutes later they decided it was time to go below deck, and the only question that remained was "her bunk or mine?" It turned out to be hers.

Barney was a happy man.

When he woke up the next morning, he wasn't sure where he was, but he knew he'd had very little sleep. He reached over, and with his eyes closed, began to run his fingers through Brianna's short-cropped hair. Ten sharp claws gripped his wrist and sharp teeth bit into his thumb. As his eyes snapped open, he found himself staring into a pair of yellow eyes in the face of a very large black and white cat. His mouth came open, but he couldn't think of anything to say.

The cat yawned, let go of his wrist, and jumped off the bunk. Barney shook the last of the sleep from his head, and still not sure what had happened, pulled on his shorts and headed up on deck. Brianna sat there calmly petting the cat.

"Where the hell did that thing come from?" he demanded.

"He's not a thing and I've named him Piper, after the famous guy who got rid of the rats. Surely, you remember the fairy tale? Well, you might also remember the wharf rat that's been plaguing us? Piper eliminated him last night. This morning I threw what was left of the carcass over the side. I've fed him scraps, off and on, for the last two weeks. He decided to return the favor and make himself useful. I gave him the leftover steak for his efforts."

"Well, I'll be damned!" said Barney.

"Probably," she said sweetly. "But unless you feel like cooking, I suggest we hit Charlie's at the end of the pier for breakfast."

"Sounds good. Okay, he can sign on, but Piper doesn't work for me. I'll enter him on the muster as RatCat."

"Oh, all right. I wasn't really happy with Piper anyway, but it was the best I could come up with on short notice. By the way, what happened to the rest of the crew?"

"I asked Melanie to find them rooms on shore so we could be alone." Barney looked at her. "Brianna, I won't ever sail on another boat unless you're there with me."

It was as close as he could come to a proposal.

"Aye, aye, mate," she said as she took his arm.

RatCat? he thought. *I can live with that. Sounds good. Yeah, that's exactly what I am.*

He preened himself as he watched Brianna and Barney head down the pier with their arms around each other and then looked up and down *Chauffeuse.*

Not bad. I guess I've found myself a new home.

He headed below to select a bunk for his morning nap.

Chapter 29

Showdown at Galleria D

AT GALLERIA D, EVERYTHING WAS in place for the gala unveiling of *Lady in Lace*. The invitations had gone out, the catering had been ordered, and the gallery was spotless. Security had been beefed up to the max. Melanie arrived early, and even though she was acting as head of security, she was wearing a designer cocktail dress. Dee saw her right away and came over to give her a hug.

"Are we secure, tonight?" Dee asked, with a smile.

"Oh, yes, everything is set," said Melanie, looking around the gallery.

"You look so beautiful; I can't believe that you're head of security."

"That's what Mitch says, and I love him for it."

"Our men do love us, don't they?"

"And we love *them*."

For the society regulars who had received invitations to the Galleria D party, it was another event on their social schedule: the unveiling of a newly discovered "Old Master." Interesting, but not earth-shattering. It was a chance to share a cocktail with friends while viewing a newly discovered painting that belonged to their old friend, Klaus.

Behind the scenes, however, things had been busy. The real *Lady in Lace* had been crated and transported from Klaus's penthouse to the gallery under his watchful eye. It was now

140

stored in a back room, under 24-hour surveillance, both human and electronic. In another room sat the forgery, which had recently arrived from the art exporter in Italy. A team of experts had gone over it, inch by inch, and had written their official report that detailed the technical aspects of the fake, including its use of modern day canvas and paints. They determined that, although it was professionally painted and closely resembled the original in style, the artist had not been schooled in the art of "recreating an old master that would fool the experts."

That afternoon, Dee wandered back and forth between the two rooms. One team carefully removed the real *Lady* from its packing crate and placed it into the elegant gilt frame selected for the viewing party. The same frame had been chosen for the forgery, and as soon as the examination was complete, it would be framed to look exactly like the original.

Leading the team of experts currently swarming over the gallery was Dee's longtime friend Eli. As Dee watched, he meticulously photographed the artist's signatures on both works of art in the gallery and showed them to her. He opened his laptop and pointed to the signatures on other Botelli paintings on display in galleries around the world.

"This is a mistake that forgers often make," he explained. "They take great pains with the painting itself, but they slip up when they copy the signature, thinking it's not important."

She nodded, studying the results more closely now.

"The artist's signature is his last name plus the year it was painted. So far, so good. Our amateur forger has done exactly that. But he or she ignored the fact that the artist formed his letters in a most unusual way. On the down stroke of each letter, see how the lines are narrow? Now, look when one of his letters take a side stroke, like the "B" in Botelli. The line is now thicker, as though the artist has turned his brush sideways and stroked it across the canvas."

By this time, he had her complete attention.

"Now, look back at our forged copy—same name, same date. Look at the construction of the letters. The lines are all one thickness; they lack the flourish that comes with the side stroke. Clearly, you can tell from the signature alone that this is not a genuine Botelli!"

Dee let out the breath she'd held ever since Eli began.

"That is amazing, Eli. Pure genius."

"It's my business, Dee. I've been doing this for almost thirty years, and I have yet to be fooled. When all else fails, look closely at the signature: it's almost foolproof."

"Tonight, at the cocktail party," she said, "I'd like you to mingle with the crowd, observe the guests, and listen to what they are saying about the painting. Afterward, I would love to hear your comments."

"Of course, my dear," came his answer.

"But, you realize, that at some point there will almost certainly be a showdown. And that is when I may need you to be my expert witness."

"Understood. It should prove to be a most interesting experience."

Dee was nervous. It wasn't what she knew—and had planned for—that was the issue; it was the unknown that tortured her. *How will this play out? Am I prepared for all eventualities? What if? What if? Stop worrying and calm down!*

She, Jared, Melanie, and Mitch had one last huddle with the security team two hours before the event. This was a chance for the Protek team to meet the local men in blue who were also staffing it. One of them was a plainclothes detective who specialized in white-collar crime. He informed them that it would be better if "the suspect," as he called her, actually "confessed to the crime" in front of the guests, and they could record her on camera implicating herself. He explained that they still had a lot of circumstantial evidence, but it would be much easier to get a conviction if she incriminated herself.

Then they finalized their roles, determining what duties the police would handle, and what Jared's team would cover, and how they would deal with the various situations that could possibly come up. They checked all the security cameras for placement and clarity of video and audio. Then they went over everything they knew about Mary Rose. She was already in town, and there were two surveillance teams at her hotel. So far, she had been to the beauty salon, and her dress had been delivered. No phone calls, nothing out of the ordinary. Simply a woman in town getting ready for a cocktail party.

Then, an hour and a half before start time, Protek's security team called Melanie. Mary Rose had shown up at the hotel bar and was joined by a beefy-looking man who was obviously a bodyguard. Should they try to find out if he was packing? Dee's own security detail passed the word around about this most recent development.

The painting of *Lady in Lace*—the real one, not the fake—was now prominently displayed on a gilt easel, located to the right of the small podium where Dee, Mary Rose, and Klaus would each make their remarks. It was surrounded by stanchions, and the painting itself was covered with a black velvet cloth that would be removed at the exact moment Dee presented the painting to her assembled guests.

Dee was well aware that her own remarks needed to be both neutral and honest with respect to the painting. She planned to praise it as a work that had been "hidden from view" for three generations, which was true, and that she and its owner were proud to display it to the public for the first time in the United States. Also true. So far no mention of Mary Rose. Then she would perform the actual unveiling and, if, to that point, Mary

Rose hadn't yet made her move, she would invite her to say a few words. Dee had advised her that she was on the program and to prepare her remarks accordingly.

At precisely thirty minutes before the scheduled start time, Klaus walked in flanked by his two best friends in the art world. All three wore broad smiles.

"My sweet," he said to Dee, "allow me to present the two gentlemen who have accompanied me tonight. To my right is Andre. You will remember him from the old days when he sponsored one of your young artists. He actually stole him out from under my nose."

Both men laughed, and Dee gave a tiny bow.

"And, let me present to you my other dearest friend, Oscar."

Dee saw a man who was obviously well advanced in age. His clothing, although elegant, could not hide the fact that it had been made for a much younger man.

"Oscar is the only one of my friends who ever met my father, and that was when we were only boys. He is truly my oldest friend."

"I am honored," said Dee.

She saw that Klaus was actually rubbing his hands together in glee as if he couldn't wait to get started with the ceremonies.

"Where is she?" Klaus asked.

"Mary Rose?" asked Dee.

"No, not Mary Rose. *The Lady*. Is she the *Lady Hidden Under the Velvet Curtain* or the *Lady in Waiting in the Back Room*?"

"Your *Lady*, the real *Lady*, is front and center, under the velvet curtain."

"Of course, yes," said Klaus, "she would have to be. When Mary Rose denounces her as the fake, she has to be—of necessity—the real one. Will we witness a *scene*? Do you think she will *throw* things?"

Dee nodded. "That's the plan." She came closer to him, almost whispering. "But a scene at the Galleria D? My reputation will be ruined even though I *do* have the real painting and not the fake. What will my guests think?"

"They will all still love you. I will see to that. And I will tell everyone that you have broken up an international art forgery ring, so you are to be congratulated."

Dee gave him a wan smile and beckoned for Jared to join them and say hello. The friendly chat continued for several more minutes until a voice that crackled in Dee's earpiece broke the silence.

"Subject approaching the gallery, Dee. All hands on deck." That was the voice of Mark, in black tie, who had joined them for the evening's entertainment.

By ten minutes after "show-time," as Klaus had taken to calling it, Galleria D was filled to overflowing with a mix of elegantly dressed art collectors and critics and uncomfortably dressed police and surveillance types. Fortunately, the guests were too busy greeting each other and selecting their cocktails to notice the disparity. They were here to have a good time, and, to them, that meant drinks first, and then chats with old friends.

Dee welcomed each individual and couple as they arrived and had a personal word for every one of them. She meant it when she said she had a special evening planned. They had no idea just how special it would be.

She had kept an eye on Mary Rose ever since she had greeted her when she arrived, but so far the woman was acting quietly and professionally. Dee noted that she'd made no attempts to converse with any of the guests. Every few minutes the waiter would bring around the appetizer tray, and she would wave him away. Meanwhile, the bodyguard stationed himself against the wall near the front entrance and watched the goings-on. Mark spotted him and positioned himself nearby.

Then, on a signal from Melanie, Dee took her place at the podium and tapped the mike lightly to get everyone's attention.

"Welcome, my friends. It's wonderful to see all of you here this evening, and I thank you so much for coming to see the unveiling of Klaus Vander Houten's Italian masterpiece, the *Lady in Lace*. Now, this painting has a wonderful story. And wait until you see what a beautiful woman the subject is. The artist, Antonio Botelli, was in love with her, and even though she was many years his junior, he considered her to be his muse."

A few people in the audience began to clap, and one said, "Let's see her!"

"I know you want to see her," continued Dee, not at all flustered, "but I want to say one more thing before I present the *Lady*. Even though Klaus is her owner, he has graciously agreed to put her on special display at the New York Art Museum for six months before he retires her to his private collection. That way the public will be able to enjoy this wonderful work of art that has been hidden from view for more than seventy years."

And, with that, Dee removed the velvet covering, displaying the magnificent portrait for all to see. Her guests crowded to the railing to look, and there were "oohs and aahs" all around.

"Gorgeous is right," said one.

"Stunning," said another.

"Oh my God, she's beautiful," said a third.

The invited critics crowded around and peered over the stanchions to get as close as they could.

"Oh, yes," said one, "it is definitely an original. Look at its use of light. Even indoors you can see how the artist works wonders with color to make it appear almost translucent."

From another: "He was the genius of portraits. No one else could paint expressions the way he could."

From a third: "Don't forget the signature—it's always a clue—and this one is flawless."

From a fourth: "The public will go wild when they see it at the museum."

Dee's guests nodded and strained to get a better view and murmured their agreement with the critics.

Near the back wall of the gallery, Mary Rose fumed and seethed, barely able to hold on to her temper until she could make her move. *What fools they all are! Look at them making idiots of themselves, fawning over a stupid painting that's nothing but a big fake. A fake I had made—and it's fooling all of the big experts in this damned stupid town!* She couldn't wait to get up to the podium and tell them all so. So what if she had to tell them that it was her own doing. She hadn't done anything wrong. After all, the painter's tiny star with two rays was located in a corner of the *Lady*'s lace dress, so she couldn't be accused of forgery, could she?

She had thought of everything. And money wouldn't be a problem, either. Dee had already handed her the envelope, so she knew she could pay her money lender tomorrow. All was well.

It is time to tell these damned fools how stupid they really look. It is time to denounce Smiling Dee and show everyone what an immense fraud she is.

Dee watched out of the corner of her eye as she saw Mary Rose make her move toward the podium. Her minuscule eye movements alerted the others in the room that the real show was about to begin. Dee stepped away from the podium to make room for Mary Rose, who all but pushed Dee with her hip as she passed by.

"Good evening, everyone," Mary Rose said, tapping the mike. "My name is Mary Rose Bennett and I'm an art dealer from Boston. Even though Miss Dee has not introduced me yet, I am the person responsible for bringing this painting before you tonight."

A few people stopped looking at the painting and clapped lightly, not sure yet if this was part of the show.

"Lovely, isn't it?"

A few more people looked up, still wondering what was happening.

"I mean, a painting as pretty as this *should* be in a museum, right?"

Now she was really turning some curious heads.

"I particularly like your *experts* fawning all over it. Gives it an air of credibility, doesn't it, my friends?"

By this time, she had everyone's attention.

"Well, the big news tonight is that I've fooled all of you—your *very* special Miss Dee who knows *everything* about art. All of her crony art critics and experts are here to back up her ridiculous claims that this is an Old Master—a Botelli, of all things."

Someone from the audience shouted, "What *are* you talking about? Sit down, lady!"

Mary Rose continued, her voice rising in an effort to talk over the rising tide of criticism coming at her from now various members of the audience.

"It's real!"

"Of course, it's real!"

"It's a fake, a phony," shouted Mary Rose. "And I brought it here tonight to show you that your wonderful Miss Dee *Milan* can't tell her ass from her elbow when it comes to art. She's a fake, too, just like this painting!"

"That's enough," shouted someone else, effectively quieting the audience long enough for Dee to come forward to take her place as hostess. She raised both arms, outstretched, and began to speak.

"Thank you, Mary Rose. And thank you, my dear guests, for your patience with our speaker."

"Put her in her place!" yelled someone from the audience.

"One moment, please," replied Dee. "Mary Rose is *right*, and she is also *wrong*. The reason all my experts agree that this is the *real Lady in Lace* is because it *is* the real *Lady*." At this point, she motioned for Helen to come forward, who did, pushing Mary Rose's painting on a rolling easel.

"This is Mary Rose's painting," said Dee to her audience. "As you can see, it is an excellent copy of the real *Lady in Lace*, and I invite my guests, especially my experts, to step forward and examine it as closely as they like."

Dee could see that Mary Rose's face was now red with indignation, but she stood her ground and glared angrily at Dee. She was not going to back down easily.

Dee listened to the experts' comments as they came in.

"Well done, it is, but it wouldn't stand up under close scrutiny."

"Good, if you don't get too close."

"Doesn't have the depth of the real one."

"Check out the signature—forgers always miss that."

"Might sell for twenty—even twenty-five grand."

"What's the point of this exercise?" someone finally asked.

Much to Dee's surprise, it was Klaus who took front and center this time.

"My dear friends, thank you all for coming here tonight. That's an excellent question, and I shall answer it."

A few clapped, and Klaus continued.

"Miss Dee and I have suspected for some time now that there would be an attempt to discredit her, so we did the only thing any self-respecting art lover would do: we set a trap." He gave a little laugh as he said it. "And tonight you are all here with us to witness the results of our efforts. In fact, the art world is always on the lookout for clever forgers—so you will be pleased to know that tonight we have *put one of them out of business.*"

There were cheers from a few of their guests, and several turned around to see if they could find Mary Rose, but she was deep in conversation with two large men, one of whom was reading her rights.

"You have the right to remain silent...."

Chapter 30

Summer's End

A<small>S IT TURNED OUT</small>, M<small>ARY</small> Rose spent only a few hours in a New York City police station before bonding out under her own recognizance. It had been a humiliating experience for her, one she hoped would never happen again. She left knowing she had a court date in four weeks, and she could not ignore the possibilities of how this could impact her future.

Despite her mighty business acumen, Mary Rose had not thought her plot all the way through—she had never considered the possibility of failure. And, as much as she hated to admit it, she *had* failed. She had failed to bring Smiling Dee to her knees. In fact, Dee's star now shone even brighter. Worse yet, she still owed Bruno, the money lender, three hundred thousand dollars, and she needed to pay him off.

The check Dee has given her the night of the party turned out not to be the three hundred thousand she was expecting, but rather twenty-five grand that the experts assessed as fair market value for the forgery. She cringed when she thought about it, and hoped Bruno would allow her to work off the debt using her weekly income from the business. She hoped his ties to her family over the past two generations would be the grease that oiled the wheel. She could never borrow the money from her father; he would not approve of what she had done. After all, hadn't she tried to "pet the cobra"—and failed?

Unwilling to go home right away, Mary Rose stayed in New York for three more days, wandering around aimlessly and trying to think of a way out of her predicament. Eventually, though, she knew she had to go home. She had now been away from Boston for a total of two weeks, and she could no longer postpone it.

When she landed at Logan Airport, her phone buzzed. It was Joseph, demanding her presence at his home—immediately. Thinking he would want a full report of the trip to Sicily, she took a cab and went straight there. Unfortunately, that was not to be the case. When she was escorted into the sitting room by the unsmiling housekeeper, she was greeted by the sight of her father and Bruno the loan shark in quiet conversation. They were sipping glasses of Chianti and did not offer her anything. Joseph told her to sit, and then he began to speak.

"So, young lady, you have had quite the little adventure, haven't you?"

Mary Rose started to speak and Joseph cut her off with a hand motion that closely resembled slicing someone's throat with a knife. She quickly shut her mouth.

"You think I don't get around much anymore? That I don't know what's going on? Well, you think wrong! I know everything. My spies are everywhere."

Now Mary Rose stood up, unafraid of her father and fully prepared to launch a counterattack.

"Sit down!"

Mary Rose obeyed.

"I know all about your little plan to trick Dee with your fake masterpiece. Bruno was understandably nervous when you did not meet your payment date, so, of course, he came to me. We put two and two together and found out about the artist in Quincy Market and your so-called art dealer in Sicily. Then, to put the 'icing on the cake'—and here he paused for effect— Jared's fancy New York lawyer called to inform me that you are 'under indictment for money laundering and mail fraud'—and he wanted the name of the lawyer who would represent you."

She started to say, "I can handle all of that…"

"Sit down!" demanded Joseph for the second time. "I am the one doing the talking."

Bruno had been observing the action closely. When Joseph realized that he was now privy to the inner sanctum of his family squabble, he called the housekeeper and told her to show him out. Now it was only the two of them, face-to-face. Joseph was ready to pull the plug on his eldest—and only surviving—child.

"Mary Rose, not only have you disobeyed me, you have disgraced the family."

He watched as she finally showed assent by hanging her head. He could see she knew what was coming. She just didn't know how far he would go.

"I have paid Bruno the full sum he is owed."

Her head snapped up; he watched as a tiny sign of relief crossed her face.

"As payment, I have taken your penthouse apartment, your BMW, and all of your gold jewelry. You will go to that apartment now, under guard, and remove the remaining personal items I am allowing you to keep."

He continued. "I have arranged for you to live where you will work. You will return to the old neighborhood where there is a menial job and a tiny apartment waiting for you. Remember Steve Milan's father? In the grocery business? You will go to work for him. You will go back to your roots and learn humility. You will take orders and learn to show respect. If you are good enough, you can work your way back up—but without any help from me."

Joseph saw that Mary Rose was on the verge of tears, but that didn't stop his tirade.

"There is one thing I will do for you," he said quietly. "I will pay for your lawyer when you go to trial. I need to make sure you get the best because the family business is at stake. But, if they send you to jail for this—and they most certainly can—I will make no move to stop them."

He watched as Mary Rose stood and began to walk toward him, her arms outstretched, begging him to embrace her. In response, he did the one thing he knew signaled rejection: he stood ramrod straight and folded his arms across his chest.

"One last thing, Mary Rose."

She stood there, in the middle of the room, waiting—just waiting.

"Do not come back to this house. It is no longer your home. I know the other evil thing you did to destroy this family—and for that, I cannot forgive or forget. Good-bye, Mary Rose. I wish it could have been otherwise."

Labor Day had come and gone. Jared and Dee had finally taken the long weekend to visit their home in Hudson. When they were in New York City they still stayed in the tiny apartment that was owned by Jared's mother. Every once in a while Dee called a real estate agent and went apartment hunting in Manhattan, but as soon as she found something she liked, it was snapped up; so after a while, she gave up her search.

The home on Blue Hill Road made up for the cramped quarters of life in the city. Dee could roam the hills and apple orchards to her heart's delight and then sit on the back terrace to watch the sunset over the pond that Jared had included in the landscaping. Now there were geese flying in at evening time, and Dee felt the peace and tranquility doing wonders for her. She loved owning the gallery, but this summer had been almost too much for her. She seriously thought that next year she would close the gallery for the entire month of August. That way she and Jared could spend time here and maybe take a trip together. She could give her employees a month's paid vacation so they could feel the same sense of rest and renewal. It's good for the soul, she thought.

Of course, this had been no ordinary summer—not with all that had happened with Mary Rose. Dee still could not believe the woman's audacity and wondered what had driven her to such hatred that she wanted to ruin her. In the end, Dee decided, it had probably begun years ago, when Mary Rose first knew of her as Steve's wife. Hadn't she, at the gallery, even referred to her as "Dee Milan?" Yes, that had to be it. Perhaps she thought that the Dee who owned the art gallery had become too full of herself and needed to be taken down.

Dee thought about all the people who had helped her unravel the plot devised by Mary Rose Benefacio, alias Mary Bennett. Melanie's entire surveillance team had worked tirelessly for almost two months. Bart's legal team had also advised her all along. He had recently told her that the art forgery charges probably wouldn't stick, but they would get her on money laundering and mail fraud. That was often how prosecutors brought down small-time hoods. Maybe some of Mary Rose's other businesses would fail at the same time.

What bothered Dee most was the time it had taken away from sponsoring new artists and developing the gallery. Now she would have to work twice as hard this fall to prepare for the holiday season, which was fast approaching. She wanted to do something special and thought about using *Holidays Around the World* as her theme for December. She thought she would pass it by Jared to see what he thought, but he always listened and then told her he was sure it would be perfect.

Then, in a joyfully creative moment, Dee decided to make the theme of her spring show *Sailing and the Ocean*. She knew Jared would love that. Satisfied with her afternoon's musings, she decided to take a nap until Jared returned from his visit with

Henry at the B&B. For some reason, she was unusually sleepy these days.

The big jet from Rome touched down on the tarmac twenty minutes early. Joseph was happy his driver suggested they get a head start. Joseph didn't often leave home these days, but today was an exception. The two old men waited on the sidewalk outside customs when Giancarlo, his timid wife, and their three small children, emerged from the building, blinked their eyes in the fall sunshine and looked around to see who was there to greet them.

Joseph stepped forward, gave Carlo the traditional kiss on each cheek, and then engulfed him in a bear hug. Then he delicately kissed Giancarlo's wife and patted the chubby toddlers on their heads.

"Come, come, my son. I am so pleased to welcome you. We have much to talk about, and there is a lot of work to be done. The business has suffered some setbacks and I am counting on you to fix all of that. In fact, let's go straight to your new apartment; everything has been readied for your arrival. I have even put the BMW at your disposal. It's already parked in the garage of your new building."

Epilogue

DEE LOOKED ESPECIALLY BEAUTIFUL THIS evening at the Galleria D's annual holiday party. While Jared stood protectively at her side, she greeted the guests as they streamed in. Invitations had gone out to clients, artists, friends, business associates, and Protek employees. Klaus was among the first to arrive; Dee had not seen him since September, and his pallor worried her. She made a mental note to talk to him as soon as the first rush had passed. Besides, she had a surprise for him, and she couldn't wait for him to see it.

Bart and his lovely young wife were next to arrive, quickly followed by Melanie and Mitch. Ellen and Irving had flown in from Las Vegas and greeted everyone they hadn't seen in several months. As the rooms filled, the buzz of talk and laughter ebbed and flowed with the clink of champagne glasses. Dee, pointedly, abstained and sipped ice water. She was eager to share her other secret with her guests tonight.

Dee's vision of *Holidays Around the World* had been carried out to perfection. She realized that people bought works of art that hung year-round in their homes, so she had chosen her paintings carefully with this in mind. The theme, as she saw it, was really the love that the holidays brought out in people, and that is what made each of these pieces so special. Her guests wandered around the gallery, admired the art and the decorations, and tasted the fine selection of food and wine.

Next to arrive were DJ and Gloria. Dee could not remember when she had seen two young people so happy! Gloria was radiant, and DJ had that same protective look about him that

Dee so loved about Jared. It was obvious they were in love, and she was so happy for them.

As soon as Dee was able to break free of the receiving line, she made a beeline for Klaus, who had claimed a chair and was chatting with old friends.

"How are you doing, my dear?" he asked, as she approached. "You know, you are positively glowing tonight."

"Thank you, Klaus; that is so kind of you," she replied. "But I'm worried about you. Are you well? You look like you have lost some weight."

Klaus lowered his voice. "Let's not talk of such things at the holidays, my dear; after the new year we will have lunch and I will bring you up to date. I think our little talk can wait, don't you?"

Not quite sure how to answer, Dee silenced her worries and moved on to her next topic.

"My dear friend," she began again, "I have a surprise for you."

Klaus perked up.

"Do you remember when the forged *Lady in Lace* was shipped over from Italy? I told you that the shipper had put another painting on top of it, in case the customs officials decided to open the crate."

"Yes, I remember; it was supposed to be a valueless, local painting."

"Surprise!" said Dee. "It turns out that the painter is an up-and-coming young artist in her own right, and while she is no Botelli, she is now recognized as the best new portrait painter in Europe, and she has graciously consented for me to represent her in the US. Moreover, I have framed this painting for *you*. It's your Christmas present!"

She saw the tears beginning to form in his eyes as she brought the painting out and showed it to him.

"It is lovely, my dear Dee. I shall treasure it forever—as long as forever may be."

Jared chose that moment to join Dee, and he had Gloria and DJ in tow. Dee hugged Klaus and turned her attention to the young couple.

"Dee," he said, as he held up Gloria's left hand for her inspection, "look at what these young people have chosen to do. I think a celebration is in order! I hope you don't decide to wait too long to get married. Congratulations, you two!"

Dee hugged them both. "I am so happy for you! Isn't it wonderful when you find the love of your life?"

She looked around the room. There had to be almost a hundred people, and each one of them meant something special to her. They were all people she had grown to know and love. This is what she had wished for, and then worked so hard to achieve. And this, she thought, is what it looks like! She stepped to the podium and clinked her glass to get everyone's attention.

"Good evening, my dear friends."

There were a few cheers from her audience, so she continued.

"I have always loved the holidays. Even when I was a little girl, I so looked forward to Christmas. But never have I loved it as much as I do now because I am able to share it with so many wonderful people."

Someone called out, "Yay, Dee!" It was DJ.

"Tonight, Jared and I have an announcement of our own to make. This spring there will be an addition to our little family. So excited to tell you we are going to be parents!"

Cheers went up, and, one by one, Dee's friends came by to hug her and wish her well.

Klaus was among the last to congratulate her, and Dee could see he was holding back his emotions. "I want to meet that baby, Dee. I so *hope* to meet that little baby."

THE END

www.ingramcontent.com/pod-product-compliance
Lightning Source LLC
Chambersburg PA
CBHW050947120626
46552CB00001B/429